NAMPALLY ROAD

Other books by Meena Alexander

Poetry

Stone Roots
House of a Thousand Doors
The Storm: A Poem in Five Parts

Criticism

Women in Romanticism: Mary Wollstonecraft,
Dorothy Wordsworth and Mary Shelley

NAMPALLY ROAD

A NOVEL BY

MEENA ALEXANDER

Mercury House, Incorporated
San Francisco

This is a work of fiction. Names, characters, places, and incidents either are the product of the author's imagination or are used fictitiously. Any resemblance to actual events, locales, or persons, living or dead, is entirely coincidental.

Copyright © 1991 by Meena Alexander

Illustrations by Pablo Haz

Published in the United States by
Mercury House
San Francisco, California

Distributed to the trade by
Consortium Book Sales & Distribution, Inc.
St. Paul, Minnesota

Mercury House and colophon are registered trademarks
of Mercury House, Incorporated

Printed on acid-free paper

Manufactured in the United States of America

Library of Congress Cataloging-in-Publication Data

Alexander, Meena. 1951
    Nampally road : a novel / by Meena Alexander
        p. cm.
    ISBN 0–916515–90–7 : $15.95 — ISBN 0–916515–82–6 (pbk.) : $9.95
    I. Title
PR9499.3.A46N36   1991
823 — dc20   90-5849
                                                                   CIP

If fire is lit in water, who can extinguish it?

Nagarjuna

CONTENTS

Chapter One   ☆ The Orange Sellers' Protest   1
Chapter Two   ☆ Little Mother   13
Chapter Three ☆ The Terrace at Night   27
Chapter Four   ☆ Laura Ribaldo   41
Chapter Five   ☆ Wordsworth in Hyderabad   48
Chapter Six   ☆ Rameeza Be   55
Chapter Seven ☆ Her Fever   60
Chapter Eight ☆ A Dark Room   74
Chapter Nine   ☆ The History Lesson   87
Chapter Ten   ☆ Cardboard City   98

THE ORANGE SELLERS' PROTEST

Ramu and I found a table at the New Mysore Cafe, with a clear view of Nampally Road.

It was early afternoon, the hottest time of day in the dry season in Hyderabad. Probably the noonday sun was literally hotter, but who could tell? No self-respecting person would be caught dead in the street at that hour, with or without the requisite black umbrella, while two hours later or three, caution wore off, and with classes letting out at the local college, the street was flooded with people.

Seated where we were, in a clean, well-lit spot in the cafe, we considered ourselves lucky to have beaten the students and the salesmen of plastic goods manufactured in Vishakhapatnam; the sellers of cheap airline tickets to Dubai; the housewives in their well-starched saris, cloth bags in hand stopping for a little refreshment on their way to the latest bargain at the SuperBazaar, whose red brick walls, though still unfinished, were studded for exotic effect with a cluster of polished stones from the local quarry where the Nizam once held his boar hunts.

Ramu had a shock of black hair he was forever pushing out of his eyes. He wore a cotton kurta and trousers of the Aligarh cut that were never ironed. I think we were almost exactly the same age, a quarter century old, both born a few years after Indian independence. I had caught sight of him on my very first day at work at Sona Nivas, the local college. There he was, a solitary figure, sitting reading under a neem tree. Then brushing the dust off his kurta, he pushed his way through throngs of students toward the cafeteria, a pile of tattered books in his arms. I was instantly drawn to him. Someone introduced us, and then it was easy enough to have coffee together after classes, or a quick dosa at the New Mysore Cafe.

Once he let on that we were born in the same year, but he would never tell me his birthdate.

"The day I was born? The month? You're asking for too much detail, Mira!"

"But why not? I've told you when I was born. It's important to me."

"But why should you know? It's not that horoscope rubbish, is it?"

He was wary now, pulling away.

I was hurt but managed to laugh in his face, so that he turned bewildered and I let the subject drop. Perhaps he was nervous that modern woman though I was, I might in a bout of melancholia make off to the local astrologer with his birthdate and mine, and try to get a perfect fit for some future that even the hot stars high above couldn't quite figure. Or perhaps it was a bold stance in defiance of augury. After all, hadn't he revolted against three maiden aunts who lived in a little village in the northern reaches of Kerala, each of whom had a separate horoscope cast for him? It was their responsibility to have this done, for a decade earlier both his parents had been killed in a terrible car crash on the crowded Kottayam-Mallapally Road during the Onam festival.

Each horoscope had predicted that it was Ramu's fate to study overseas. To do that, one of his aunts whispered to the others, he would have to travel to a little island in the gray ocean somewhere north of the great Godavari River. But the predictions continued: before his departure, lest a dosham, a malign influence, take hold of his days, let him marry a young girl of compatible family, born under the star of Tiruvathera. When the news was brought to him, Ramu was filled with rage.

All this he confided to me in the months when our friendship blossomed. On receiving the message from his aunts, he turned down the Rhodes scholarship that others might have killed for, accepted a modest grant from Jawaharlal Nehru University and swore on the memory of his dead mother never to leave the boundaries of free India, never to reveal his birthdate to any woman. His final year as a Ph.D. student in Delhi coincided with the beginning of the Emergency, when our khadi-clad, iron-fisted Prime Minister—she of the immaculate lineage and Swiss schooling, who on her New York trips made small type in the *Times* by buying her mascara from Bergdorf's—abruptly withdrew all civil liberties and drafted antiterrorism bills that could throw any citizen in jail without overt reason.

Ramu was active in the protests during that time, and he helped produce the underground newspaper that students set by hand, moving from house to safe house in the rocky terrain around the university. Several times Ramu was detained and held in custody but let out after a few days. In December of that year he was offered a job at Sona Nivas College, part of the Central University of Hyderabad. We met in February of the new year.

Those first days Ramu took it upon himself to show me around the library, the cafeteria, and the cashier's office where at month's end we could pick up our resplendent salaries of one thousand and one rupees: quite enough for a single person to take care of board, lodging, books, a few movies, and even the odd meal out. One morning he introduced me to the New Mysore Cafe and Bolaram, its plump owner. One sultry afternoon a week later, when classes were abruptly cancelled for a political meeting the Chief Minister had announced, he showed me the path to take, past flowering magnolia, through maroon seeded grasses, to the lotus pond that was tucked away to the side of the Public Gardens, just a stone's throw from the railway station at one end of Nampally Road.

"If you come early enough, at the crack of dawn," he explained, "even before the mist clears, you will hear all these little pop-pop-pop sounds. Tiny explosions from the water. The lotus buds popping open!"

He smiled at me then, somewhat tenderly, and I, unable to bear the feelings that welled up in me, set my right hand in his. We stood like that by the clear water for a long minute before moving on.

It was also from Ramu that I learned how to press myself against the college wall to avoid mud from the motorcycle convoy that always preceded Limca Gowda, the Chief Minister of the state. Limca Gowda was an ambitious man and wished to turn himself into an absolute ruler. Hyderabad is in the Deccan. It is the navel of the subcontinent. "Codpiece to the heart," as a local poet dubbed the city in a drunken fit, a reference to its foundation several centuries earlier by Muhammad Quli Qutub Shah, who, filled with longing for his beloved Bhagmati, she of the fragile dancing hips, was struck with the notion of founding a city in her honor.

Subcontinental spaces being vast, Hyderabad is a respectable distance from the republic's central seat of power in the north. Still it was one country, and the ironfisted lady provided a clear model for Limca. She in turn saw in him an ally she might well manipulate to consolidate her own rule. The notion of unquestioned power vested in a single man pleased him enormously. Sometimes at night he dreamed that he was the old Nizam of Hyderabad, returned in new flesh to claim his kingdom. On those mornings he awoke bleary-eyed and had to be restored to his senses with a double dose of martial music played by his Ever Ready corps on bassoon, tabla, and a squeaky violin, a cast-off someone had borrowed from a great master of the Karnatic mode of playing the instrument, who, having been invited to the United Nations to play with Yehudi Menuhin, left his house in

Madras in his wife's care. She was a third cousin of Limca's wife's brother-in-law, and on hearing of the difficulties the Chief Minister had in awakening, picked up the old instrument and silently passed it on.

Music or no music, Limca Gowda knew that it took man's greatest efforts to secure power. His party, which had been voted in four years ago, now ruled with an iron hand. Dissent was strongly discouraged.

As my friendship with Ramu blossomed, I sensed the torment in him. He wanted to make a difference, to do something for India, whatever that something might be. His grandfather had been an associate of Gandhi, and Ramu, brought up in strict boarding schools, felt his new life as a college teacher to be the perfect starting point for action. After all, reading Marx and Habermas took one only so far. After his hectic life in Delhi, Hyderabad seemed almost unreal. But this was where he was, and he had to begin. As he confided his dreams to me, I felt that my life, our lives, were all around in the acts and movements of countless others, waiting to be known. There was a quiet joy in me then, an expectation.

That afternoon in the New Mysore Cafe I inched my chair toward the table, to get as close to the window as I could. Ramu had gone to the bathroom, and as I waited for him I noticed how the newly installed plate glass was speckled with bits of grime. Each fleck was distinct, as if fragments of eggshell had stuck there, and in the spaces between, I could see into the dust haze rising over the tarmac, high as the palm trees in the compound far to the right.

I let my fingers rove and felt a crack in the marble-topped table. Rather a large crack. I could feel the food that had fallen in and grown stale. When Ramu came back, he leaned forward and touched my hand. I felt the dampness from the water on his fingers. Somehow we did not need to make conversation and so sat companionably looking out onto the street. I noticed the splintering sides of the wooden shack where a passerby could buy cigarettes, singly or in the packet, or find beedis with their bitter-flavored leaves and bright pink threads. Beyond the shack, on the other side of Nampally Road, were stone steps leading to the CLS Bookshop.

The flower seller who squatted on the steps was suspended in a pool of light. The roses in her plastic bucket were pocks of sheer color, pink and yellow and a stale, burnt white. I wished I could sit closer to Ramu. Behind us was the clatter of tin spoons and plates. Suddenly platefuls of steaming idlis were thrust forward. A delicate flavor of steamed rice filled my nostrils, then the pungent scent of sambar flavored with a little too much asafetida.

"Thank you, Bolaram."

The hotelier leant forward: "How's the sambar?"

I nodded, not quite in the mood to make remarks about his new cook. He stood still, his checkered tray cloth tucked under his armpit. He seemed puzzled as he stared into the street.

"Seems very quiet, don't you think?"

Ramu nodded absently, then straightened up in his chair.

"See that woman? No, not the flower seller. Behind her."

A little to the left of the steps ran a ditch that in monsoon season was always filled with dirty water. Now it was bone dry. Next to the gully was the still unfinished wall of the SuperBazaar. I saw a head darting past a pile of bricks and grimy red stone where the wall stood half broken. It was a woman, her hair well oiled, tightly tied back. Her mouth was open. Then all I could see was a flat orange cart pulled up so that the wheels at the back were at the very edge of the gully.

"Behind the cart, see?"

Bolaram was still there, craning forward now. "Orange sellers," he said. "It's the new tax, kills them."

Someone summoned him and he moved away reluctantly, his damp tray cloth over his shoulder. Ramu whispered, "Keep looking, Mira, carefully now. We must use our eyes."

The cart glistened in the sunlight as the haze swept off Nampally Road. I squinted through the thick glass and made out the empty wooden surface. But no, it wasn't quite empty. There were clusters of dead tamarind leaves tied together in a knot to ward off the evil eye. I sensed a gentle stirring. A brownish cloth slipped off. I could make out a child, probably a year old, its belly swollen. Its right hand was opening and closing, clutching at the air. It struggled to sit up. Its mouth and eyes were visible now. It must have been wailing, for suddenly the woman slipped her hand out of the ditch and rocked the orange cart.

The metal wheels slipped. I could make out the mother's body steadying the cart as best she could. I was so intent on watching the mother and child that I did not see the street filling up. Slowly, ever so slowly, as if we were all cupped in a dream, flags spilled over the surface of Nampally Road. First a dribble, then a rush of red flags held upright, brandished in the air. A hundred men and women, no a hundred and fifty, two hundred, raised themselves from behind walls and ditches and poured in from the crossroads. They grouped behind a banner. Three men held it aloft. "Orange Sellers of Telugu Desham" it read.

A woman ran in front of the three men. She had a pile of oranges clutched in her arms. She cradled the fruit against her ribs as she ran. The people started to march behind her. But they had barely started when the motorcycles appeared, bearing straight down on the orange sellers. The first one buzzed like a gnat, its black body gleaming, headlights glinting in the heat. Then fifteen or sixteen, like a whole horde in formation, crashing through the unarmed men and women. The riders in their khaki uniforms were armed with lathis. They were Limca Gowda's special branch, the Ever Ready men. Each had a torch in his waistband. Each of the motorcycles had its headlights on, the bulbs donated by the Union Carbide people in return for favors received.

The Ever Ready men leaped off their machines and started beating the orange sellers, dragging them to the pavements, kicking them. The orange sellers were scrabbling free, their banner torn and bloodied, running as hard as they could until the street resembled a ditch of water in which living creatures were immersed, struggling for their lives, their arms and legs damaged by the blows falling from the iron-tipped lathis.

I thought I caught a glimpse of the mother hidden in the gully, the child wrapped in her sari, the orange cart with the tassel of tamarind leaves smashed by boots and lathis. She had taken the child back for safekeeping, back as close to her own flesh as she could. And now she was running.

Quite close to the cafe door a man had his head bloodied, half broken by the iron. Bolaram pulled him in with the help of several customers, washed and bound his cut. I saw three women dragged by their hair, tugged by their armpits into a waiting police van.

It was all over fairly soon: the peaceful demonstration that had not even started, the savage interruption, the cries and blows, then the whirring sirens and the backfire of motorcycles starting all over again.

A quarter of an hour later the street was empty of people. All that remained was torn clothing, broken stones from the unfinished wall and smears of blood, a dark wetness on the asphalt.

Suddenly ten motorbikes returned, their headlights blazing. Behind them was a glistening Cadillac, a bit of unreal chrome and steel in the suffering world, a surreal irruption. A window rolled down. A right hand loaded with rings waved mechanically. As the driver speeded up, the car swerved to avoid a broken orange cart. The tires crushed a plastic bucket against the wall. The roses that had remained, shot into air, a shock of lavish color from the petals, a fragrance no one could seize. Then the car was gone. Its occupant had vanished.

The next morning I saw the flower woman, a bruise on her cheek, rocking back and forth on her knees. Her bucket was empty. As she rocked, she held onto the remains of a cart. By the sentry box at Sona Nivas College, just a few yards to the right, was the rest of the cart, the broken handle, part of a wheel, and a torn banner, blood colored, smeared with dirt.

☆ ☆ ☆

Durgabai rubbed her nose with the back of her hand, a slow, anxious gesture.

"So what was all that about, child? I heard the racket when I turned by Mirror Mahal."

Tired after a long day's work, she rested her feet on the back of a dining room chair. It was Tuesday and she always had late hours then. It was twilight in the courtyard. Dusk fell on us all, the rich, the poor, the battered, the wounded, those of us who were hungry and those who fed well and easily. Fireflies circled the tulasi bush. They made tiny sparks of light, a nocturnal version of the flame Rani lit each morning by the stone pedestal where the bush grew, part of her daily ritual. In the stillness I could smell the musk from the rose flesh. The heavy white bloom trembled under the running tap. Someone was washing her hands.

There were small, everyday noises from the street: the stir of traffic, the bicycle boys crying to each other, the banana seller haggling with customers, the apothecary dragging in the metal clock with the image of Queen Victoria on it, then shutting up shop. We could even hear him coughing. Things were that quiet in the aftermath. It was as if the bloodshed in the afternoon already belonged in another country.

She lifted her hand and smoothed back a hair. I heard her watch, a man-sized one, still on her wrist, beating its heart out.

"So?"

She was waiting for my reply.

"It was awful, Little Mother."

"Ramu told me something about it. I stopped the car on my way home. I passed by the cafe, you know. I saw him there. The road looked bad."

I could see she was trying to help me on. But she wanted to hear my story.

"We were in the cafe having a coffee together. People appeared suddenly in the street. It was a morcha, quite peaceful, carefully planned, I think. There was even a tiny child left by its mother on an orange cart by the SuperBazaar wall. Where else could she have left it?"

I wiped the sweat off my forehead with the edge of my sari. I was finding it difficult to go on.

"There was at least a truckload of policemen after the Ever Ready men arrived."

"Someone must have tipped them off."

"Of course."

I continued. Now I wanted to tell her what I could. "A man had his head broken, quite close to where we were. Bolaram pulled him in and cleaned him up. I wonder if he'll ever reach a doctor."

I fell quiet, thinking of the tiny child I had seen on the orange cart before the morcha started.

"That small child, Little Mother, it was just a baby."

A sudden light fell across her eyes. A curtain had blown loose and the fading sky shone into the room.

"When was it? Last Independence Day? Remember when you came with me?"

☆   ☆   ☆

It was Independence Day, August 15. National flags flew everywhere. I accompanied Little Mother to her clinic. Hand on the horn, she drove her gray Fiat through the twisting streets of the old city. She could race and swerve and stop, she could avoid children with their sticks and balls, old rickshaw men, buffaloes, bicycles, dogs, cats, creepy crawly things that rose from the waters of the Musi River and edged into the street. In half an hour flat, we were by the Dolphin Press. Behind it, I glimpsed the corrugated metal roof of her clinic.

The whole clinic was not much more than a longish room bisected in two. There was a small waiting area and then the room where she did her work. The two were separated by a green cloth strung from a line that ran from wall to wall. Already people were lined up waiting for her: coughing children, feverish children, children plagued by nightmares, women with itches in the wrong places, women with irregular bleeding, women who heard whispers coming from their wombs in the dead of night. She treated them all as best she could, each according to need.

The man was already there when we arrived, a tall man with a turban wound around his head in the manner of those from the hill country. His body was lean, exhausted. He held a burden in his arms, a child, perhaps ten or eleven years old, wrapped in a blanket. Siki the nurse had the day off, so it was my task to help Little Mother carry out her doctor's kit, open the windows to let in light from the street, make sure water was set to boil for sterilizing needles. All the while the man stood there patiently, following us with his eyes, saying nothing. His gaze was filled with an odd fatigue, or was it sorrow? When I drew aside the green cloth, for it was time for patients to come in, he entered first and tenderly laid the child on the metal bed. Covering the child's head was a stiff brown cloth. Slowly the man pulled the cloth away.

It came off and with it came some putrid, cream-colored stuff. Where the boy's forehead should have been there was a huge hole. The skull was torn away at the top, and whitish brain matter was visible. I clutched the window ledge and in spite of myself bent forward. Little Mother was leaning over the child. Over the soft, juggling spheres of his brain, over the tissues of knowledge and desire, maggots crawled, fat white maggots.

They dipped and crawled, they danced in the blood that dried at the edges of the skull. The father just stood there.

"What's happened, man? You have to tell me." She was washing her hands now, in preparation, drying them on the flecked towel that hung on a nail. The boy stirred a little. His foot trembled, then fell rigid. His eyes were shut tight. He had long, black lashes. The mucus from his eyes had hardened, lengthening the lashes. I never saw shut eyes so beautiful.

The story tumbled out in the rhythmic speech of the hill people. It was many weeks now, three or perhaps four. A leopard had mauled the boy. The father, a widower, had done his best—cow dung, mudpacks, bitter herbs boiled according to the prescription from the vaidyan in a neighboring village. Finally in desperation as the infection poured through the child's head, the man had carried him, walking the whole way, the fifty-odd miles into the city. Quite by chance someone by the railway station had pointed out the way to the clinic. The man had no money with him, just the clothes on his back and his dying son.

She pulled on her plastic gloves and gently touched the child's head. Using her tweezers she started work, lifting out the maggots, each bloated with the boy's blood. She set them in a kidney-shaped pan by her elbow.

In the car on the way back, I was ashamed of myself. A mixture of hot tears and vomit had forced me out onto the clinic steps. I had hung there, fingers clamped around a pillar as the work of minimal healing went on. Little Mother was silent for a while but turned to me as we crossed the bridge, with the black river waters beneath us.

"That child won't survive. I had to tell him. The brain was far too damaged. It's a wonder the child held on for so long."

☆ ☆ ☆

Now we sat in the half darkness, each filled with memories of a brave child with a head wound. I mused on the baby in the orange seller's cart. It probably lived in a hovel at the edges of the city. Free medical aid, however minimal, was available. If that infant survived into childhood, grew to the age of ten or eleven, what would become of him or her?

I heard the milkman at the gates. He always rang his bicycle bell at least twice in short sharp tinkles. I rushed to open the inmost gate in time to prevent him from shouting out, in a rough, singsong voice, "Rani, arre Raniamma," a lyric that always irritated Little Mother. She got up when I did, hurrying to wash the brass vessel into which the fresh milk was to be poured. It was Rani's task, but Rani was nowhere to be seen.

CHAPTER TWO

LITTLE MOTHER

I had found my way to Durgabai's house quite easily. Five thousand miles away, in the Midlands, I had received detailed instructions, and they did not lead me astray. I still had the map in turquoise ink, folded now, propping up the crooked leg of my writing desk.

One cold foggy morning in late autumn, flourishing the letter of appointment I had received from the Vice-Chancellor of the Central University, I'd made my way to the flat where Siddharth lived. It was a poky little place on top of a pawnshop in a run-down side street not far from Nottingham Playhouse. I displayed the thin oil paper and the envelope complete with stamps worth several rupees, all pasted down with rice glue. I pointed out the bold orange lettering that ran across the bottom, "On India Government Service."

"I'm legit now!" I sang to Siddharth, a brilliant, shy lad, a few years older than me. His girlfriend — the blond, lank-haired Vanessa — was curled up in a corner cradling his sarod.

"I'm going to Hyderabad, your natal place, no?"

So it was. And Siddharth broke open a fresh bottle of wine, instructed Vanessa to reheat the rabbit casserole so I could have a taste, and sat down concentrating hard, giving me directions on how to reach his mother's. He omitted all the bits about plane and train and bus. After all, who needed that stuff? He concentrated on the footpaths.

We sat there as the whistles blew in the depressed Midlands factories, men raced over the slag heaps and new, half-finished highways, and children circled the run-down cafeterias in the day-care centers Mrs. Thatcher had nearly destroyed.

"Remember when we first met?" I quizzed Siddharth, as Vanessa frowned at me from the middle distance.

"You were in that student protest shouting 'Mrs. Thatcher, Milk Snatcher! Mrs. Thatcher, Milk Snatcher!' over and over again. She'd just cut the milk for the school lunches. Your voice was quite hoarse. And now, imagine, you're giving me directions on how to reach Nampally Road in our own country!"

Siddharth smiled a little wistfully. His research in some arcane field of mathematics was falling apart. It was not his intelligence that was in doubt, rather his application. For each morning on waking, Siddharth sat cross-legged at his sarod, positioned its brown globe against his bare feet, and started tuning the ivory-colored strings. Often he lost himself for hours in his playing, and the fact that his grant was running out did not deter him in the slightest. He'd met Vanessa at a local concert he'd given and she had clung to him ever since.

"Not a word to my mother about all this," he cautioned, flinging his arm out.

"About us you mean?" Vanessa lisped.

"Well that too."

"Promise!"

He was pleased then and drew me down to look at the map he was drawing on a folded sheet of paper torn from an old calendar. He pencilled in a large roundabout with crossroads running in five directions, the fifth being the Y made by the stout arms of Abid Road running north as it forked at the central post office of Hyderabad City. Nampally Road cut across Abid Road.

"Turn left there, it's very simple. You'll be walking in just the opposite direction to Sona Nivas. Aai's house is just a stone's throw away. She'll be delighted to see you. Walk straight down past the spectacle shop and on the other side, just as the street narrows, you'll see a huge peepul tree. Really you can't miss it. Are you following?"

"Of course."

I glanced at him. He seemed a little nervous now, as if the act of drawing the map had drawn him closer to his own home and all the expectations lodged there. After all, he was the eldest son and his father had long been dead.

"You won't get lost, will you, Mira? I know how bad you are at such things!"

Vanessa was tittering now and this annoyed me no end. So I said nothing and let Siddharth continue.

"In any case you won't miss the peepul tree. Just behind it is an immense iron gate. The gate is cut into three parts. Three sections swing open depending on the size of the traffic. Viz., mere man, or man with sarod, man with sarod and Vanessa, man with sarod and Vanessa mounted on a white horse!"

We were all laughing now in sheer delight, and I left a few hours later, full of rabbit casserole and table wine, clutching the map.

I called on Durgabai as soon as I got to Hyderabad several months later. Siddharth had already written to her saying I'd be arriving. She drew me into the living room, delighted that I had come with news of her eldest son.

"Of course you must live here, child," she insisted. "Look at this great house all empty now except for me and Raniamma. All the bedrooms are shuttered. Why not take the room on the other side of the courtyard, just across from me. That way we can all keep each other company. And you'll be so close to work."

I could not refuse her generous offer. I insisted, though, that I pay her each month the small sum of three hundred rupees, just about enough to cover my meals. That was all she would accept. As the days passed and we grew fond of each other, I found it hard to imagine living anywhere else in Hyderabad.

As befit her age, I addressed Durgabai as Little Mother. Though Siddharth had hinted at her professional life, he had given me no details, and I was amazed that she worked as hard as she did. She was obstetrician, gynecologist, and pediatrician all rolled into one. On some days her job was to deliver babies. Out they poured in a dark, mucky stream of life and blood and hot cries.

"A new India is being born," she whispered to me between patients, scrubbing her hands with red carbolic soap.

With the young children, it was vaccinations or medicines for fevers and boils. With the women, it was women's business, aches in the ovaries or breasts, bleeding or the stoppage of blood, care for the tiny embryos as they grew in their mothers' wombs. For women in trouble, raped or saddled with an unwanted pregnancy, all it took in the early stages was a quick D and C as it was called, dilation and curettage.

"Then you have to build up the woman's spirit so the shame doesn't last," she explained to me. "It's terrible, the fate of some of our young girls."

☆ ☆ ☆

Durgabai had inherited her house. Built around seventy years ago by her father, a physician who had done well serving the late Nizam, it was a large house with whitewashed walls, set around a courtyard. The old doctor had ended up as the chief court physician. Now the grand days of the house were over. In the upstairs quarters the velvet-backed chairs and brocade-lined screens stood huge and mute under their dusty sheets. Tiles were cracked in the courtyard. Paint had chipped off the shutters or ran in little streaks down the walls after a series of rough monsoons. The city had grown up around the house, and Nampally Road, which was once fairly quiet, had turned into a noisy thoroughfare.

Durgabai charged practically nothing and still used the run-down clinic with a tin roof in one of the poorest parts of town. Its great distinction was that it stood next to the Dolphin Press, well known as the site of all sorts of theosophical publications. Why, even the great Annie Besant had visited the press once, Little Mother told me.

"Rather a plump lady with those black pressed skirts she always wore. I was a child then and hung around the steps with all the other children staring at her!"

Now ants, chickens, and, in the monsoon season, frogs from the ponds in the public parks ran up the steps of her clinic and leaped onto the pillars of the Dolphin Press. Clearly Siki the nurse had to make do with very little in the way of amenities: a single metal bed with a piece of cloth that was taken off and laundered as often as necessary, a wash basin with a leaking tap, a hot plate with a stainless-steel double boiler in which the syringes and scissors and other such medical implements were boiled.

For thirty years now Little Mother had practiced medicine and in all that time the thought of moving her working quarters had never occurred to her. Some of her students, less scrupulous than she, better able to sniff out where the money lay, had installed themselves in air-conditioned minipalaces, fitted with spittoons and automatic dispensers of betel nut and chunam. Sometimes they passed Durgabai in the street or on the steps of a grocery store, or at a rich man's wedding. Each time they felt a slight unease. She in turn was troubled by their "show," as she called it.

"Why are they doing this, child?" she would ask me in puzzled fashion, as we sat taking tea and biscuits, which we sometimes did on the hottest afternoons when she was forced home for a little break. The ceiling fan with its silvery blades turned the lukewarm air. The windows were only half shuttered, and a green light from the peepul tree fell in through the curtains.

"What do they hope to gain? What can our India gain? In any case, child, who can afford it these days if not with black money?"

Black money was illegal money. It was the currency of smugglers and businessmen from the Gulf. It poured into the country.

Secreted underground, it wrecked the economy. No deals could be tied up without it. It ran the world of the rich, it choked the rest of us. To Durgabai it was a kind of poison that was fouling the land. Much like the poison in the hoods of Kaliya, the mythic serpent. One morning at breakfast, raising her voice just a fraction so that Rani would hasten in with the tea, she confided in me.

"I am waiting for Lord Krishna. He must press his tiny feet on Kaliya serpent, subduing it. How else can all this poison be spilled out?"

For Little Mother there was no gap between Krishna's world and ours. The earth, however dry and racked with heat, was the same for all creatures. And time was all of a piece. Still, Durgabai could hardly be accused of spending her days waiting for Lord Krishna, devoting herself to singing prayers or fasting. She scarcely had time to rest.

Outside her house she had a sign painted in black letters. Visitors often knocked their heads against it as they bent past the gatepost, stooping to enter the miniscule gateway whose intricate openings and systems of swing latches and rusty bolts took years to master. The sign read:

Durgabai Gokhale, MD. Gyni-Obstetric.
Bombay University; Diploma Univ. of South Wales
Head, Hyderabad Center for Children's Diseases (Retr.)
Thirty Years of Service — Welcome all

The sign faced Nampally Road, and beneath it hung a wooden board with her address: 4.1.347. Next to the gatepost where the sign hung, grew the great-shouldered peepul tree Siddharth had spoken about. The shadow of that tree fell all the way across the street and cooled the apothecary's shop. I can still see the precise pattern of shade made by the pointed leaves as they flicked and tossed across the street and over the shop, darkening the heavy plated silver clock that stood just outside.

The arms of the clock were buried in the skirts of a queen, a painted lady. VICTORIA, it said beneath her in bright silver. Her cheeks were like apples from the Gulmarg Valley. Her skirts were gray like fog over the Thames. The apothecary had inherited the clock from his uncle, who had been Compounder to the Resident. The clock struck at noon, scaring the crows in the banyan tree and agitating the old men who stepped out of rickshaws in search of bits of dried root, rare herbs, and gold dust to cure all manner of ailments.

Once an old man who had come a great distance stood in front of the clock face. Hearing the din, seeing the gray skirts shake on the queen, he started trembling and could not stop. The very next day the apothecary, on Little Mother's advice, covered the clock in a length of green cotton. Cuffed and masked it stood at midday under the sign that read "Long Life Apothecary." For three paise a piece, one could lift the cloth and see the glazed eyes, the stuck crown, the clock arms moving on a surface as pale and listless as the buried side of the moon.

Just to the left of Little Mother's house was a barbershop. To the right was a bicycle shop. The bicycle man had thirty apprentices, small, thin boys aged five to twelve. At night they wrapped themselves in rags and slept on the pavement. The peepul tree shielded them from the harsh glare of the street lamp. Durgabai took great pleasure in treating their various ailments: coughs, shivering, toothaches, stomach cramps. With the offer of lollipops she enticed them into her clinic so she could vaccinate them in due season.

During the day Rani left the outer gate open so that the bicycle boys could work at the edge of the courtyard. Often I saw a child of five learning the craft with great concentration, shoving spokes into the inner rim of a wheel, polishing a bumper with a moist rag, learning to mend a puncture. I once asked Little Mother if they had parents.

"They were all picked off the street. He's a good man the bicycle fellow. He treats them as well as he can. But they eat so poorly. A bit of rice, or roti and some dal if they're lucky. I have dreams of keeping a buffalo to provide them with milk. What do you think? By the bathroom, in that plot of grass just under the Ribaldos' window?"

She smiled. We both knew that the space there would scarcely do for a buffalo. The Ribaldos lived just behind the dentist's office, squashed between our kitchen wall and the decor of Sagar Talkies, the premier theater of Hyderabad.

☆   ☆   ☆

The morning after the orange seller's protest the street was unnaturally clean. It had been hosed down during the night, and it looked almost as it might have on a normal Tuesday. But there was an empty spot where the flower woman had sat on the steps by the CLS Bookstore. A curious antiseptic smell pervaded the air and quantities of water laced with milky disinfectant pooled in the gully by the college walls. Then, too, someone had clearly taken a broom to the bloodstains by the roadside where several orange sellers had fallen, so that no trace was left of the violence. People gathered together in worried knots, and even the predictable arguments about the test matches lacked their usual vivacity of tone. The left-wing students were puzzled by the brutal attack. How could it possibly help Limca's image, particularly with his birthday celebrations just a month away? Had an overzealous Ever Ready colonel taken matters into his own hands? The students seemed particularly troubled that morning. It was rumored that several Ever Ready men in plainclothes had infiltrated the cafeteria and student union building and were listening to conversations. As soon as he saw me that morning, Ramu rushed me off to the shade of his favorite neem tree and muttered, "Keep quiet, Mira. Ask me nothing. There are meetings I must attend."

His attitude infuriated me, but there was little I could do. For scarcely had I uttered a word in question before he vanished, racing out of the gates. As I walked home from work that afternoon, it seemed to me that only the crowds that poured into Sagar Talkies were their usual selves. Or was that just an illusion? It was the first night of *Isak Katha*, the multimillion-rupee theological film based on the life of the young Isaac of biblical fame.

Word was out that the highlight of the movie was the moment when out of the tangled locks of poor Sarah—played by the fabulous Mumu all decked out in mud streaks for the occasion—leaped a ram. Out of those locks, out of that maternal brow maddened with grief at the thought of losing her only son to the knife, leaped a full-throated, bleating ram recently trapped from somewhere near the wilds of Golconda. It was the genius of the Telugu cinema to disguise Mumu, who desperately needed a comeback as the passionate, seventy-year-old Sarah. Mumu was still best known for her role several decades ago as a hennaed dancing girl in the "Typewriter tick-tick-tick-tick" song-and-dance routine, where skimpily clad she danced on the giant keys of a make-believe typewriter. Perhaps this brand-new theological film would seal her fate, make her a household word again. All this had been patiently pointed out to me by Rani, Little Mother's cook and general helper.

But when I walked in through the gates the morning after the orange sellers' protest and called out for Rani, she was nowhere in sight. Instead, much to my surprise I caught sight of Durgabai's friend, old Swami Chari from the nearby ashram. He was dressed in his fraying lungi and juba. His legs tottered a little. As he was about to trip over the metal ledge of the gate, I put out my hand and held him lightly by the elbow.

"Up there, there, up there."

I glanced up into the branches of the peepul tree, but he was pointing at the gatepost. He seemed oblivious to the large stream of people just behind us, struggling to push forward into the gates of Sagar Talkies.

"Namaskaram, Swami Chari." I bowed low. "Are you all right?" I ventured to add, feeling a little foolish. He pretended not to hear me, or perhaps it was indeed true, as Little Mother insisted, that her old friend was hard of hearing.

"I keep recommending a hearing aid, Mira. There's a new Australian kind that's been donated by the Shriners. It fits quite comfortably into the ear. But he's so stubborn."

I thought of her words as the old man, seemingly deaf to the goings-on around him, pressed on with a tale drawn from the recesses of his memory. In the manner of those unused to interruption, well pleased by the sound of their own voices, he spoke as he might have written, in a narrative suited to distant listeners, their own voices annulled, their whole souls compressed into the orifice of a delicate ear.

"Up there he crouched, the drummer at Durga's wedding, all got up in muslin and a brocade waistcoat. Drumming up a frenzy. By the time the bride was ready to enter the ancestral gates, the poor man was dizzy with his own sounds and clung to a branch for dear life. In she walked, through a swarm of children, a mist of them, hundreds with rose petals in their hands, and some with silver jugs, sprinkling her with rosewater. Just as the bride passed, the drum dropped with a little thud. And the drummer hung there pedalling his legs in the air as if the rush of wind might bear him up. How shy she was, the veil shimmering over her. I don't think she even noticed the thud behind her, poor child. A love match. Did you know that?"

We walked slowly through the outermost of the three gates. I saw the barber's assistant peer out. His hands were all soapy. He was watching me, wondering what I was doing with the old man. He ducked when he saw the swamiji peer up. He dropped his soiled hands into the hot water and winced.

The old man was in a talkative mood. I helped him over the second gateway.

"Durga's mother was dead set against the marriage. You know that don't you? Unsuitable family, a slight history of madness there. But the girl would have nothing but marriage with this man. How fierce she was. I can see her standing in this courtyard arguing with her mother.

" 'The times are changing, Aai,' I can hear her say. 'A hot wind will blow.' I tell you the old lady was worth her salt. Sat in her armchair, under an umbrella, taking it all in, not flinching. Recognized a bit of herself in the girl, I think. It was the height of the Quit India movement. All that energy released. Durga had her way."

We passed through the tiny doorway into the courtyard, stooping a little. I felt a flood of pleasure at the cool stone tiles, the colors softened to a slate blue with sun and water. All around the edges of the courtyard grew a tangle of lemongrass. By the water tap was a mass of rose petals, wild and turbulent. I could sniff their hot scent from where I stood.

I led the old man into the drawing room. I was weary from a day's teaching. Durgabai was nowhere to be seen and I could not leave him alone, half deaf, brooding.

"Rani," I cried out. "Rani, Raniamma!"

I had to repeat myself over and over. There were chaotic sounds in the kitchen, the ungoverned clatter of pots and ladles, a tinny sound as if a knife were scraped against a stainless-steel dish.

"Rani, the swamiji is here."

She stumbled in heavy and floral, shiny with sweat, her nylon sari slipping its folds. She must have weighed three hundred pounds. I could tell that a visit from the swamiji pleased her. Rani was known to have metaphysical urges, and one of the swami's sermons had helped her a great deal. As I called out for her, I could almost hear her voice in my ear explaining the effect of his words.

"It was the sermon that ends with the soul as a swan, *hamsa,* you know. Rising. Rising. Listening to him I felt just like the white-winged swan painted on the street wall of the ashram. I could have kissed his tiny foot. He was so good, better even than a swamiji in a movie!"

Rani fed herself a heavy diet of movies. Each morning, after washing the breakfast dishes, she would set off next door to Sagar Talkies to take in a matinee. The film stars—Mumu, Baby Shireen, Dharam, Jehangir—tumbled through her thoughts. In her dreams she was awakened by Akbar, the rage of the Telugu Talkies, sipping at a milkshake, winking at her. In rare moments of despondency she hastened to the ashram. Her work at home was light, so she had the luxury of cultivating herself as best she could.

How gracious she was now, bowing. Offering tea and biscuits, sitting at the old man's feet and drawing him out. I felt the swami was in good hands. He could defend himself if need be. In any case he had known Rani a long time. Twenty-five years. For as long as she had worked for Little Mother.

She had come as a grown girl from an orphanage when Little Mother's eldest son was born. Durgabai was alone with her parents. Her husband was away in Glasgow earning a higher degree. Then the whiskey caught him. No one was quite clear what happened after that. Was he stoned to death in the Gorbals, as Ramu whispered to me? "An early version of their race riots, you know." Or did he fall over a cliff as Rani had it, or off a ship in a drunken fit?

Once after her day's work Durgabai told me her story. It was one of those days when she had been up for forty-eight hours at a stretch. She was almost sixty, but she still persisted without sleep.

"Dysentery cases, child. One after the other. One case of suspected typhoid. A caesarian. Then all my lectures to the young mothers. Over and over again. I give them the same routine on basic hygiene. Washing the baby's loin string."

She'd insisted I accompany her to the clinic just to demonstrate the condition of the black thread tied around an infant's loins. She picked up a loin string as it hung against a plump little belly. The black string was smelly with urine.

"See what I do? I take scissors and cut. Simple as that. Takes away the evil eye, you say. Well, I reply, woman, this urine-soaked thread is no good for your child. This is modern India. Did we fight the British for this? Did we gain Swaraj so your child could catch an infection?"

I might have been a young intern, preparing for a bout in the villages. She wanted to show me life. But that evening after supper, as darkness poured in through the courtyard and the music of *Isak Katha* rose from Sagar Talkies and mingled with the cries of rickshaw men, sellers of mangoes, and peddlers of cooked channa, she slipped into an easy chair and mused about her dead husband. It was a life lived so long ago she might have been recalling someone else's story.

"He travelled from Bombay on a ship called *The Trafalgar*. I felt so proud it was called that. So real somehow, out of an old history book!"

She sighed, curling her toes under her sari as she sat in the wicker chair, her cotton sari shot with little blue flowers draped over her generous thighs, her tired chest and arms.

"It happened on the way back. He was returning home. At least that's what I thought."

Now there was a slight quiver in her tone.

"It was a stormy night, and they were just three hours out of port. The ship keeled over to the side. He was strolling on deck. Washed off. Washed off without a trace. They sent back the small bag they found in his cabin, his few odd papers and things, a pair of spectacles. The trousers, suits, medical books, the new equipment he'd bought for us was all coming in the holds. They sent it to me. The spectacles are here."

She pointed out the little cupboard behind the statue of Ganapati, the round-bellied elephant god. He who opens doors all over the universe, and shuts them too in people's noses.

"If the boys ever return and need anything, it's all stored there. Safe and sound. I used to hope that Siddharth would wear those spectacles one day. Silly, isn't it?"

She stopped. We could hear the crickets in the courtyard, the louder croak of the bullfrogs from the wastewater that pooled in the graveyard behind the house. The music from the talkies rose as if someone had turned the switch incorrectly, letting the volume of sound rise in a sudden crescendo. But after a moment the sound subsided, giving way to a cacophony of lorries, hooting, one after the other, as if Nampally Road had suddenly grown very congested. Then for a split second all the noises stopped. Just the cicadas making their electric trill as the walls of the house seemed to quiver and drop, inner and outer dissolved into each other.

She bent forward listening intently. She listened to almost everything in this great noisy city. Her hands lay on her sari, loosely, one on top of the other, the blue veins visible at the wrist.

"How still it is," she said. "Child, I feel I can almost hear your heart beat."

She laughed a little, as if to calm herself, then picked up her story again.

"I think his drinking started after the episode in Burma. All those years in a Japanese prisoner-of-war camp. His brother was captured too, and died of starvation. Probably there was torture involved, but Kailash would never speak of it. When his brother died in the camp, Kailash lifted him up in his arms and buried him. He scooped out sand with his bare hands to make a grave. A Brahmin suffering without cremation, just buried like that.

"Then his mind worked loose. He was brilliant of course, and his medical training never deserted him. But when he came back to me he needed to drink. I found him what I could. I thought the trip to Scotland would help."

Abruptly she raised a fist to her eyes. She was trembling.

CHAPTER THREE

THE TERRACE AT NIGHT

The following morning, I woke before dawn, and for roughly half an hour before the sun dashed the courtyard into tiny glittering tiles, I sat quietly at a small wooden desk trying to keep to my usual ritual. My window looked over an abandoned muslim graveyard. I could see a few goats chewing sticks, a crow hopping in the bleached flat stones that marked the graves. In the middle distance was a tamarind tree, and just behind it, a break in the wall. Beyond the wall was Nampally Road, curving round past the post office and the small Shiva temple where all the beggars congregated on Tuesdays.

I sat at the window, looking out, trying to write down a few words on the long sheets of lined paper I had bought from the stationer's. I noticed how the color of the lines was much the same as the color of the tiles in the courtyard when water splashed on them in mid-morning. I listened intently for the

27

little boy who sometimes wandered into the graveyard with a pile of sticks or bits of torn tire under his arm. I would wave at him. If the sky was clear and the sun very hot, his hair rippled, the black turned to a radiance that dissolved in the air. I loved to see him then, his hair all light and his small hands picking through the stones for what he could find.

Though I tried I could not really write my story. Each time I tried to write, everything splintered into little bits. I could not figure out a line or a theme for myself. The life that made sense was all around me in Little Mother and Ramu and the young students, the orange sellers and the violent and wretched, ourselves included. It was all already there. No one needed my writing. It could make no difference. I had seen the same policemen who beat the orange sellers over the head, riding bicycles in a general strike a year ago, their right fists raised. Many of them were desperately poor. They needed a pay raise.

As for the Indian past, what was it to me? Sometimes I felt it was a motley collection of events that rose in my mind, rather like those bleached stones in the abandoned graveyard the boy picked his way through. I had no clear picture of what unified it all, what our history might mean. We were in it, all together, that's all I knew. And there was no way out. Once I had tried explaining this to Ramu, but my way of putting it made no sense to him.

"Its because you're so immersed in this writing thing, Mira," he complained. "It doesn't let you turn right or left. And what do you do with it, after all? Look at all those notebooks under the bed!"

He pointed at the neat piles of notebooks I had arranged on a tablecloth under the bed, rolling the cloth over so that the dust would not catch in the frail leaves of paper.

"At least I keep Muhammad Ali in business!" I tried to turn it into a joke. Muhammad Ali was the stationer who sold me the notebooks at a special price because I worked at Sona Nivas. Unlike Ramu, he was most sympathetic to my needs and would spend long chunks of time picking out the right notebook from the vast quantities of old stock he had stored at the back of his shop.

"But then I've never asked him to read anything I've written. I think I did recite two lines to him once, and he said it sounded very like a ghazal."

Ramu, though, was no longer listening to me. I think he was nervous about the fact that I spent long hours staring out of the window and jotting down odd thoughts. And I was fearful that the odd lines I read to him must seem the mere fruits of bourgeois privacy, though he was too delicate to say so. But what else did I have as a starting point? What truth would there be in me if I tried to slough that off?

I had come to Hyderabad after four years as a graduate student at Nottingham. When I began my English sojourn I found myself at a great disadvantage as far as the loneliness of life was concerned. I suffered from dislocation. Somehow I had not gathered into myself the resolute spirit needed for solitary study. In my own way I slowly picked up courage. The first year, rather than immerse myself in faded volumes of PMLA, I conducted experiments on myself. I went to all-night parties with ear-splitting music and blinding lights. In daylight, in company, I tried to eat with my left hand.

I had been taught from birth that the left hand must never be used for eating. The right hand is the hand that is visible when rice is held to the mouth. I am naturally right-handed but as part of freeing myself, tried to eat with the polluted left hand. After all, the left hand was as much a part of my body as the right and nothing to be ashamed of. My awkwardness was put down to general social ineptitude. A brilliant child, but out of place in the Midlands, I heard Miss Foxglove whisper. She was the unmarried older daughter of the Warden in the Hall of Residence I lived in. She gave me little lessons in poise, how to hold my knife, how to gobble tidbits, how to wash them down with wine.

I did these things as best I could but felt myself a great mockery. On the one hand, no one valued my experiment in left-handed eating for I confided in no one. No one, that is, except Siddharth who understood perfectly what I was about. Siddharth's music made a great hole in him, so with Vanessa's encouragement he had entered into a guru-chela relationship with a local swami. The swami was a plump, overfed adolescent boy who had been born in the foothills of the Himalayas, then brought to England by his mother who had formed an alliance with an Englishman and now worked as a stenographer for the local county council. At the age of six the child had developed soul power, as the mother Sheela-mataji put it. By the time he was thirteen, the boy wonder was installed as a new avatar, and his portrait, complete with pink tongue licking an ice-cream cone, adorned numerous walls in Nottingham, including the walls of the pawnshop beneath Siddharth's flat. Jaguars and Mercedes Benzes rolled around to the modest council house where the mother and son still lived.

Each morning after playing his sarod, Siddharth used to go to take darshan. It hardly fazed him when the child-guru was caught by the Indian customs service and charged with smuggling in watches and minute electronic parts used to create instant vihbuti in his oversize waistcoat.

Siddharth still insisted that I was foolish to go it alone. "You need a guruji, Mira," he kept saying.

I do not think he realized the staunchly secular nature of my enterprise. After all, who in the whole of the Midlands could tell I was naturally right-handed? Transcendence had nothing to do with it. At the same time, however, the strain was becoming too much to bear. I felt my nerves all jangled with the effort. I was trapped in the effort to remake myself and all the Husserlian epistemology I studied, flat sere stuff filled with post-Cartesian precision that respected no one's soul, did nothing to help.

The job offer in Hyderabad could give me a way out. I returned to India determined to start afresh, make up a self that had some continuity with what I was. It was my fond hope that by writing a few poems, or a few prose pieces, I could start to stitch it all together: my birth in India a few years after national independence, my colonial education, my rebellion against the arranged marriage my mother had in mind for me, my years of research in England. How grotesque I had felt, how cramped and small, tucking myself day after day into a library seat, reading up on my chosen authors. Now in Hyderabad I was fully adult. In any case my mind had grown stronger. I could live my life.

When I had finally begun to write my thesis back in England, I had argued implicitly against the experiments that I conducted on myself. I had been forcing myself to go out each night with a different fellow so I would never get attached, to leap up and down or twist and jive at the student mixers with those harsh strobe lights and deafening music that was all the rage, to drink more than I felt comfortable doing, and to smoke until my throat hurt. All this was on top of the left-hand, right-hand stuff. My thesis, though, had an essentially conservative bent that troubled other parts of me.

In writing it seemed to me that memory was essential. Only memory, I argued, and the continuity it provided could pull the voice together. One of the poets I read very closely on those cold winter nights back then was Wordsworth. Now I taught his poems at Sona Nivas. They were part of the set exam for the M.A. finals. When Durgabai, who had read the daffodils poem but not much else, asked me who the poet was, I explained that he had written several poems about returning to places that he loved; that he was ridden by guilt after abandoning his French mistress and baby; that he was a great poet still, haunted by memory. I thought one of his descendants had become a postal clerk like Jagdish, her brother's nephew who lived in Amaravati. Another of his descendants I thought had travelled to India and become a school inspector in Bambrali. And as distances go, Bambrali was not so terribly far from us, just a day and a night by train.

It was not so long ago that I had felt Wordsworth should be my model. He understood suffering; desire that could not let itself free. Why couldn't I write with that clarity, that precision of feeling? I had forgotten that the Wye Valley poet hated crowds, had no conception of the teeming, boisterous life we lived. The lines between inner and outer he valued so deeply were torn apart in our lives. That distinction had dropped into the ditch where the broken orange cart lay.

But still the old model held me in its grip, and I was stuck as a writer. When I managed a sentence or two, my words made no sense that could hold together. The lines sucked in chunks of the world, then collapsed in on themselves. Our streets were too crowded, there was too much poverty and misery. The British had subdued us for too long and now that they had left, the unrest in rock and root, in the souls of men and women, was too visible, too turbulent already to permit the kinds of writing I had once learned to value.

In any case, those who heard of my poetical ambitions thought this writing business a great eccentricity in me. And I must confess I felt slightly ashamed, as if back in my own country I had been caught eating with my left hand. Once Ramu, in a curious mood, tried to console me.

"Look here, Mira. I know you have those notebooks hidden under the bed. But we all have our skeletons, don't we? So long as you don't impose what you have on the public sphere, its OK. Know what I mean?"

His studies in social philosophy made him seem more rigid than he was, and his words made things harder between us. I resolved to forget the whole matter as best I could and live as a creature ready and willing to renounce her addiction to the written word. But it was easier to make that resolution than keep it, especially when I was all alone in my room.

I was surprised when Ramu walked in so early that Wednesday morning. Little Mother had already gone to work and I imagined Rani had carelessly left the little gate unlatched. Instantly he noticed my pieces of paper and bottle of Quink. Clearly he was distressed at the idea that I should even consider writing at a time like this.

" 'Poet, be seated at the piano,' " he mocked me gently.

"Where does that come from?"

"You should know. I have always disliked that poem." Then he added, "The poet who wrote it was an insurance man. Hoarding it all up for eternity. The horror of it! The upshot of the poem, which I really can't quote, is that even when stones are thrown on the roof, and bodies are carried in the street in a time of great trouble — consider us now in Hyderabad — the poet should sit there writing. It's stupid, Mira. It doesn't make sense. As you know, someone like our poet Sri Sri is totally different. He drinks a lot, but that old man is totally committed."

I felt irritated as I listened. It was not that I disagreed with what he was saying, just that my poor efforts didn't really merit all that excitement. I wanted to tell him that, but I didn't. I crumpled up the top sheet of paper.

"Ramu, I am twenty-five, but I hardly know what I'm writing. I'm so tangled up inside with all that Wordsworth and Husserl and English education. What am I to do? You know that I can't go home now and have mother marry me off. I can't be washed clean of all my thoughts, be dressed up in silks and pearls and tiny gold slippers, married off in grand style to an engineer or an estate owner. Even if mother pulled it off, I would never survive. The old world is blowing up in our faces. Great Aunt Chinna is finding it harder and harder to tick off names in her little black book. 'So few good families!' "

I mimicked her voice, a low croak.

" 'And when the boys go off for studies they barely return, or if they do, bring back white women, or divorcees, or Punjabis or Paharis. As for the girls, they refuse everything. Aaaiee, what's to become of us?' "

I stopped. I held my breath. He was sitting at the edge of my bed watching me intently. He had grown thinner, I thought, in the last few days. His blue shirt was all crumpled, the sleeves rolled up in the heat. I wanted to be finished with my speech. I wanted to sit close to him, saying nothing, nothing at all.

"Ramu, I'm here, that's all there is to it. Can't you accept that? I too am part of it all. Like the SuperBazaar and the Mirror Mahal where the shoppers go, like the orange sellers, even like the policemen. As for what I might write, it's not even worth a moment's thought."

I stopped short and stared at him. By now my hands were clenched and my weight against the small writing desk was hurting my back. I could hear the little boy with his sticks outside in the muslim graveyard.

"Nothing will come of it. So why even say anything? When have I written a line that you've found pleasing or thought well of?"

"Look, Mira, you know I don't care if you write."

I could tell he was on the defensive now.

"But you do, you do. You can't bear it. Little Mother's different. She just takes it as part of me. I hate your saying all this."

"What have I said? I just quoted a line you couldn't identify. Listen, it's an American poet. Why don't we go out? Let's stroll down Nampally Road, OK?"

He tucked my arm into his and I let him. I was not wholly unhappy to leave my room and the small pile of blank paper.

✩　✩　✩

The walk did us both good. Later that night after our classes were over I took off my sari for him. We lay down on the cool stone floor in my room, between the metal bed with its mosquito netting all tied back with ribbons and the small desk where my pen and paper still lay. We made love to the sounds of the crickets in the orange tree. From time to time a bird circled the gravestones, or a pack of fireflies hung in the tamarind tree. There were no stars as yet to be seen out of the window. Little Mother was out for the evening, and Rani had taken herself off for a visit to the ashram. Ramu and I had the courtyard to ourselves.

We took a long while. I felt his ribs and counted them over and over with my fingers. He held my breasts close as if the weight of his body might cover me entirely, take us both down through the cool stone into another kingdom. I think we were both happy. Afterward we walked through the courtyard in our bare feet and climbed the staircase to the terrace. The staircase was dark. I shut my eyes, guiding myself with a hand on the rail as I climbed. He was just behind me.

On the terrace we stepped over the pipes that carried water down into the house. We walked past the water tank to the very edge of the parapet. Just three feet away, slightly higher than our heads, was the painted facade of Sagar Talkies. I could have unravelled my sari, floated it like a pale flag, and it would have touched the little pink bulbs at the top of the Sagar Talkies Facade. SAGAR was spelled out in large English letters. We heard the hum of the projector inside and the hubbub of moviegoers. In a few minutes the crowds would swarm out of *Isak Katha*.

I pulled Ramu away from the parapet wall. I did not want any passersby to see us. We moved backward, feeling our way hand in hand to the shelter of the peepul tree. The great tree that stood by the gatepost rose as high as the terrace and higher, its topmost branches curving downward to make a canopy of green over the corner of the terrace. The leaves were packed close enough to ward off sun or even a light drizzle. We sat there under the cool stars, hidden by the shelter of the green night leaves.

He put out a hand and touched my hair. It was quite long in those days. I did not look at him. I let my eyes open out to the darkness. The sound of the crowd pushing and pulling, thrusting out in a great flurry of arms and legs, entered my ears and took over. I was that sound. People were thrusting out of the pink painted doors of the cinema theatre, flooding into the street. The rickshaw men and the taxi men were shouting. The private cars and buses were hooting loudly. Everyone was shoving outward.

Later, when the sounds had quieted down a little, I knelt by the edge of the parapet looking out. In the distance toward Gowliguda the factory lights flared, crimson and white, almost like the ebbing flare of fireworks. The river had dissolved into the darkness.

Suddenly a spew of lights shot up, off its surface. It was someone's wedding on the waters, in a boat. They were letting off fireworks. Closer at hand, cutting through the street sounds was the wail of keening, sirens, then ordinary human voices raised at night. I could smell the unrest, a faint whiff of tear gas. But where were the sirens coming from?

☆　☆　☆

Early the next day Ramu and I went walking down Nampally Road. As we crossed by the apothecary's shop the morning sun fell on our faces. On the same side of the pavement was the Optical Palace. Outside it, hundreds of spectacles of all sizes and shapes dangled from threads. They refracted the light in a thousand rays so that if you could look into each and every one of them, at the very same instant, the whole world might be visible — sky, trees, clouds, the fiery sun, the massive pulsing street.

Beyond Optical Palace the road narrowed a little. We hurried to cross by the Gandhi statue. There was a slight break in the traffic. As we raced, I heard the voice of the blind beggar behind us. He seemed to be running too.

"Amma, paise do," he called. "Amma, amma!"

I could not stop. Ramu was pulling me away from a truck that hurtled toward us at great speed. Now we stood in the traffic island, right in the middle of Nampally Road, in the shadow of the Gandhi statue. We were safe there, at least for the moment. Behind us was the post office. Forty years ago several men had been shot on those steps. It was during the uprising. They were fleeing British soldiers. Their bodies were dragged through the streets by the mounted police, as a sign. Only one had escaped in a trail of blood. Invisible arms had drawn him into the safety of a house on Nampally Road. At dusk he was carried off in a covered boat down the river, into the marshy lowlands south of the city.

What became of him? If he had been a young man now, where would he be? I was thinking all this in my head, as the streets narrowed and the lanes grew darker. I held onto Ramu's arm as we jumped over puddles, avoiding the tiny squawking chickens that ran out of Feroze Gandhi Park. Suddenly the land opened out and we stood in front of Gowliguda police station.

We leaned against a tree and looked into the building. Very little was visible, just the whitewashed front walls, the pillars and pointed roof. Inside there were policemen moving about. As for the two small jail cells behind the main room, who could be there? Or were they empty?

"Mira, there's some talk a woman is being held here. In the smaller of the two cells."

"Why?"

"I heard it from Chellapa. Some say it's a woman called Rameeza Be dragged in here by the police. Just wait a minute."

He pushed me behind the tree trunk and made off up the steps. A cur dog followed him, its tongue hanging out. Crows, their feathers a brilliant black in the heat, scattered noisily as Ramu walked up the steps. I saw him go in the swinging doors, but it was evident he had not gotten very far, not even as far as the main room. In less than a minute or two he was out again, and behind him were two policemen arguing noisily. Ramu shouted something at them, waved his arm, and headed back toward the road. He did not want the policemen to see me. He walked deliberately in the other direction, toward a small pawnshop. I stepped out and followed him. The policemen were staring at me now. Behind us, a jeep pulled into the drive and a man in a white shirt and starched dhoti jumped out. The policemen jumped to attention. It was obviously a politician, one of Limca's followers, but why was he here?

☆ ☆ ☆

"You know what I think? That woman Rameeza is in there, in the cell, and they've done something to her, I'm sure of that. Those men were so nervous when I walked in."

Ramu leaned over the parapet. Down below the bicycle boys were giggling over a film magazine. Their heads were polished, almost metallic in the street lights that shone down on them.

"I'm sure she's there."

"But why, Ramu, why would they keep her there? Unless they have something to hide?"

He was angry now, I could tell from the sudden tightness that hit his body. We were so close that another inch and our skin and bone might have been welded together.

"Of course they have something to hide. They always have something to hide. And now our civil liberties are being removed, bit by bit. What can't they do? Under the new terrorism act put out by the central government, you or I or Durgabai, any of us could be dragged off to Gowliguda jail or worse, for

indefinite incarceration. No real reasons given. Didn't you hear?
Or don't you listen to the news? Even the Vice-Chancellor is
worried. All his light-in-the-darkness bit falling apart. Poor old
fool."

I rather liked the Vice-Chancellor. He was in his mid-sixties
now, a little bent with the cares of office, but still given to
publishing editorials in the *Deccan Herald* on the role of education in the modern age, on what a young student, always a
generic male in these articles, can or can't do for his country. His
favorite set piece was on how the university was really a light-
house in the midst of a raging storm. It was the Light in the
Darkness. But even he realized that his rhetoric sounded tinny in
the new Hyderabad. After all, what could stand in the way of
Limca's mad ambitions?

Fully authorized by his own ruling party, Limca Gowda had
decided to turn his dreams to good use. His office was now run
from the old fort of Golconda, the seat of the rulers of ancient
Hyderabad. It was rumored that for his birthday celebrations fast
approaching now, he would take hold of history with an iron
hand, mix and match as he desired, dress up as the last
Qutubshahi, and mimic the mad gestures of the dead Nizam.
One of my students whispered in my ear that the curator of the
local museum had been forced to draw detailed patterns of the
Qutubshahi's clothing, complete with patterns of brocade and
cut of velvet ribbon, so that each garment could be replicated for
the birthday celebrations.

It was no secret that Limca Gowda was extremely anxious
about the great popularity of the previous chief minister. NGR,
as he was known, had been the idol of the silver screen, and his
popularity with the villagers could not be easily rivalled. Now
NGR was dead, felled by a massive heart attack suffered in mid-
air as he was flown to Switzerland for a rest. Limca Gowda, astute
as ever, spread rumors of huge secret bank accounts, kickbacks to
Scandinavian firms for contracts for the new irrigation projects
being developed with money from the World Bank. He had
wangled his way into office without too much difficulty, but still
anxious and insecure in his heart of hearts, Limca Gowda longed

to be as popular as his dead rival. At all his public gatherings, to inject a tone of levity and at the same time to calm the hordes of secret service men who surrounded him, Limca Gowda drank bottle after bottle of the soda that bore his name: Limca Soda, a lime-colored drink notorious in the region. The public was awestruck watching the Chief Minister, soda dribbling down his chin, his stout body surrounded by secret service men all decked out in three-piece suits and black sunglasses modelled on Papa Doc Duvalier's dreaded Tonton Macoutes.

Twice, due to the bad water used in the soda's preparation, hundreds who had consumed it at a wedding had been forced to go to the hospital with cramps and violent vomiting. Since the Limca company was owned by his son-in-law, the very next day at a public gathering the Chief Minister made sure he was photographed holding a bottle aloft. It became a fashion then to drink the stuff. The price for each bottle was raised by ten paise, but still the sales grew.

It was no secret that in his bid to consolidate power, Limca Gowda had gathered around him a crack corps of secret police, the Ever Ready gang as they were popularly known. They ran his office. The Ever Ready men were suspicious of the Vice-Chancellor with his liberal ways. Once the old man had refused to shut down the student newspaper; refused even to censor editorials highly critical of the way money was being spent on the grand archways and glossy platforms that rose up, at enormous expense to the taxpayers, like an elaborate stage set, beribboned and painted, around the railway station or airport any time the Chief Minister was travelling. And since the ironfisted lady often summoned him northward for consultations, the swelling cost of these erections never subsided.

The very day the orange sellers morcha had been put down, the students issued an ironic, fierce denunciation of the Ever Ready men who always supervised these elaborate cover-ups. After all, in the interests of chief ministerial hygiene the public spaces had to be freed of all riffraff, beggars, and other assorted ill-bred characters. And the Ever Ready men had to be on hand in case anyone protested the right to remain. The piece was entitled "At Our Own Gates." The violence was coming closer. In half an hour the newspaper sold out. At the same time piles of Limca bottles were found smashed in the student cafeteria, and no perpetrators could be found. All this was a prelude to the troubles that were spilling out from Gowliguda police station.

In the darkness, standing by the terrace ledge, Ramu was making plans.

"They can't afford any trouble before Limca's sixtieth birthday celebrations. He exhibits himself so rarely in public now. But he'll appear, if necessary well guarded, dressed in whatever paraphernalia he pleases. If that woman has indeed been raped and is still there, in police custody, they might do anything to her, absolutely anything. They can't afford a hubbub now. Not with the opposition parties gathering all over the country. Not if she's still alive."

In the darkness as I listened to his voice, I searched out the place where the river should be. To the right, where the river curved around to the bridge and the dome of the museum was just visible, I saw a small fire blazing in the water.

A fire lit in water, was it possible? What could it be? A mess of oil, a sheet of tarpaulin drenched in kerosene that someone had flung off the bridge? But who would do such a thing? I pointed out the small flare to Ramu. He followed my gaze and caught it just as the sharp flames fizzled, dissolving without visible remnant into black water.

I shivered. Suddenly the whole world felt cold. I saw her eyes, the eyes of the unknown Rameeza, black as the deepest pools in our river, filling me, sucking me down into a world from which there was no escape. Ramu drew closer to me. He could feel my body sometimes as if it were his own. He covered my hand with his. Both my hands with his. We stood there, as if we were two branches of the peepul tree that grew outside Little Mother's gate, bent downward, earth colored. If only we could have stood like that forever, on a cool night terrace, high above Nampally Road.

CHAPTER FOUR

LAURA RIBALDO

I could not sleep that night. I was troubled by bad dreams. Was there really a woman locked up in the police station, curled in the mud on the cell floor? Who was she? Would she speak to me? I felt my mind was tearing apart. I could not force my thoughts round to the Wordsworth poem I had to teach in an hour's time. All those words on a page were so far away. What did he know of our world, our pain? I thought I might have a word with Little Mother before she left for work. More often than not she was able to calm my thoughts, return me to the realm where actions made sense and lives were lived out with compassion and common sense. But by the time I got dressed she was already in the bathroom, having her morning wash.

I could smell the smoke from the water she heated with neem twigs and dried branches of the old coconut tree that stood between us and the small flat the Ribaldos occupied. Only Rani was visible, sulking a little. She darted forward with surprising agility, a small coring knife held upright in her hand. Little Mother called through the steam that blew from the bathroom window:

"Mira, listen my child, I know you have early classes today. I have barely had any sleep. A C-section late last night. Did you hear me come in?"

She did not wait for a reply.

"Will you do me a favor? Our Raniamma deliberately left the lid off the dahi pot to spite me. There were four black ants in there this morning. She knows my people are coming from Koregaon."

I glanced at Rani's face. She seemed dangerously close to me, knife in hand. Next to her feet was a bowl of uncut tindals, our supper if we were lucky.

"Run over to Laura's and ask for a cup of dahi. There's still time to make a new batch. I'm not foolish enough to send Our Lady over."

I was uncomfortable with her request. She had no idea what my night had been: how I had tossed and turned, imagining Ramu next to me, his cool fingers covering my breasts, circling my mouth. Then the dark irruption, the eyes of an unknown woman breaking into the circle of desire, her mouth wide open in a noiseless scream. Suddenly all I could see was the door of the police station swinging shut and Ramu's right hand caught for an instant in sunlight.

Thinking back I figured out that it was a repetition of experience, what I had actually seen the day before as I stood in the shadow of a tree outside Gowliguda station. Why hadn't I gone into the police station with Ramu? Was it cowardice? Was it the old trick of femininity, hanging back a little until the coast clears? But hadn't he prevented me from going forward by saying, "Mira, you wait here, wait for me here"?

Would those words haunt all my nights? All these thoughts were tangled in my head as I stood next to Rani with her coring knife still held bolt upright, in utter silence. Little Mother started to repeat herself, then opened the door a crack, letting out the fragrance of coconut oil and soap.

"Child, did you hear me?"

I straightened up. "I'm going Little Mother, just now."

"Take a katori with you, so we don't have to return Laura's cups and lids."

☆   ☆   ☆

I disliked visiting Laura Ribaldo. She was our most proximate neighbor and Rani's best friend. Laura and Rani shared a whole world: a fantasy life built on films and the life of film stars. They learned all they needed from twice-a-week visits to Sagar Talkies and a close scrutiny of *Stardust,* the tabloid that revealed the intimate lives of the stars. They shared a taste for synthetic clothing and bright sugary drinks. In each other's company, at least once a month, they visited the local Catholic shrine or the ashram by the river, it scarcely mattered which.

The last time I had seen Laura she was walking into the distance, leaning on Rani's arm. Laura was terribly thin, and her habit of dressing in black lace for those infrequent visits to holy places, brought out her pallor all the more, made her bones stick out, until her very body seemed an insult to health. Her friendship with the corpulent Rani may have been based on a curious bodily symbiosis that no one else could grasp.

Unlike Rani, who was satisfied with the comforts of her daily life, movies, sweets, odd bits of silver or stainless steel she stole from Little Mother's pantry and sold for the price of two nylon saris, Laura was gripped by a desire to flee Hyderabad. Henry might have had something to do with it. Sometimes he beat her about the ears so violently she was forced shivering and half naked onto the balcony that jutted out from their flat.

Laura's three sisters were in Canada. They wrote her letters filled with news of shopping malls that were palaces of chrome and plastic, crammed with glittering things to buy, carts that you pushed through aisles as music rang in your ears.

"Why, even the vegetables there are covered in plastic," Laura exclaimed to Rani. Rani, who did not quite believe this, had asked me for confirmation. It seemed hard enough to believe. In Hyderabad we stored our plastic bags with great care and washed and hung them out to dry so that they could be used over and over again. As a mark of great friendship Laura presented Rani with a plastic bag from Calgary printed with the logo of the Red Onion Supermarket. Her sisters had sent her some nylons, a pot of rouge, and a long-lasting lipstick in the bag. Now the bag was used for Rani's collection of *Stardust* magazines and hung on a nail below the stone stairs that led to the terrace.

☆   ☆   ☆

Laura's bedroom was very dark. The thin red curtains she had patched with darker material let in little light. What came in was tinted with the color of the cloth and made bedding, dresser, and chair seem overblown, part of a colorized movie in which the heroine, forced into the red light district, finds it impossible to move out and stands there, rigid and forlorn, half acting, half feeling her way to that part of her life that had led her up the rickety steps into the darkened red room.

I was struck by the way in which each of the four legs of the dresser stood in a rusty tin of water. One normally did that with a meat safe in which food was stored. Laura caught me looking down.

"It's sweet, Mira. The face powder Mimi sent me from Calgary. What did you think I kept there! I don't want the ants to get to it."

I believed her. There was a pack of ants down below, pooled over a scrap of moist pallid stuff that probably passed for face powder.

"Calgary's so cold, it freezes over in winter, river and all, the roads freeze too, can you believe it?"

I smiled. I did not want to be rude. As politely as I could, I held out the katori for the small amount of dahi I needed.

Laura relaxed. She didn't have to prove herself to me. She could be gracious to a fault.

She rose quickly from the edge of the bed, straightened her taut black hair, glanced nervously at a framed image of the Virgin of Calangute that hung above the mirror.

"That's my Virgin, you know?"

"Yes, Rani told me."

"If I ever get to Calgary she'll be with me."

The image was framed in cheap plastic: the Virgin of Calangute. Her lips were pressed tight in precise brush strokes, the mahogany-colored brow lucid in the half light, a bluish tinge to it as if a vein beat violently under flesh making a life abrupt and feverish, cutting at the cheap means of mechanical reproduction. There was gold foil set behind the dark neck of the Virgin. As if in supplication to some unseen god, her fingertips were folded under her pointed chin. The paint had smeared over the nails so that they resembled Laura's own well-stained ones.

Once the Virgin had been worshipped with incense sticks, the slow sway of censers. There were lavish hymns, cries of the faithful. More recently, on full-moon nights she was celebrated with raucous laughter by leather-clad motorcyclists. They had swastikas painted on their forearms. Daggers made of blunt iron hung around their necks. They tossed bottles of discarded beer into the churchyard, almost cracking the window next to the niche where the Virgin was housed. Cigarette butts were tossed in, the odd condom, a few empty syringes.

One night the faithful of Calangute broke in through the ranks of motorcycle men. They dashed into the open church and lifted the Virgin off the wooden wall. In great haste she was borne off to a lesser-known nave in the Cathedral of Bom Jesus not far away. And there she rested, attracting large crowds. Many made the pilgrimage each week from Calangute: black-veiled women, men who had known pain in love or ignominy in labor, children dragged along by their families, tongues working over tight wads of toffees, cheeks streaked with sweat. They reached out their sticky hands to touch her and the Virgin was pleased. There was a gold light in the alcove where she hung, a light distilled from the sandstone in the cathedral walls.

Laura's mother had turned to the Virgin in her day of need. Struck down with terrible pains in her womb, she had sworn lifelong devotion if the child were born normal. Laura had appeared, all twenty inches of her, bone thin and perfect, except for a right foot that was twisted slightly out of shape. She grew up in the shadow of the Virgin, and on her mother's death carried the reproduction that now hung above her mirror from room to room until Henry had found a mechanic's job in Hyderabad and settled the family in the two-room flat next to Sagar Talkies.

Laura was fetching the curds for me, chattering away about Calgary: how there was no dust there, Mimi said, no ants or crickets to speak of, just asphalt and chrome and plastic. I tried to imagine the Virgin in the cold Canadian air, hung on a nail above a metal bed, while in the morning light Laura dressed herself in tights and nylon pants and a cheap sweater, tugged on her boots, to ready herself for work.

"Mimi is babysitting now," she cried out from the kitchen, as if catching my thoughts.

"Very lucrative, she says. Better than hiding in the room all day and praying to the Virgin."

In my hurry to get back to Little Mother's with the katori full of precious dahi I tripped over a rug and Laura had to rush forward on her high heels to steady me. Thanking her, with what dignity I could summon, I inched my way down the rickety stairs until I reached solid ground. Ten feet above me she stood like a dark cutout, her skirts blowing wildly in the sudden wind, her palm extended as if in a curious benediction.

"Come again, come visit again," she lisped.

I did not linger, I had to get to Sona Nivas in time for my class. After depositing the katori at home, I grabbed my small cloth bag filled with books and papers and hastened past the Gandhi statue. A long line of red buses arriving from Golconda forced me to stop for a few minutes. I glanced up at the stone feet, just level with my eyes. It was Gandhiji. He too had become an icon now, yet how much closer he was to us than the Virgin of Calangute. But what had we made of him?

Just thirty years ago Gandhi had been living and breathing in this world. There was no need then of stone statues. "Father of the Nation," it said in Devanagari script under the high pedestal. Above, the smooth shoulders were hunched forward as if to resist the wind or help his body along. He held a narrow walking stick in his right hand. His eyes, polished lovingly by the sculptor and washed with years of sun and rain, stared into a future that had disowned him. What would he have made of us, our lives fractured into the tiny bits and pieces of a new India? Our thoughts were filmed over with so many images that the real no longer mattered: the march on the street just a day ago, or the rape of an unknown woman, could vanish into thin air, and someone like me could stand in front of a class with book open, mouthing unreal words. I felt my chest tighten at the thought of students crowding into the small lecture room to listen to me.

CHAPTER FIVE

WORDSWORTH IN HYDERABAD

The classroom was a makeshift one, a converted bedroom in what had once been the home of the poet Sarojini Naidu. The window at the back was plugged up for painters who had to dangle from the scaffolding trying to fix plaster. There was no lectern. Folding metal chairs borrowed from the cafeteria were placed in a semicircle. The rim of the semicircle grew larger and more disorganized as it spread outward until the very edges of the room seemed to burst with the burden of students making small talk, putting out cigarettes, straightening their hair or spectacles while they waited for me to start the day's work. I pulled my sari tight around my waist and cleared my throat.

To gain courage I glanced at the students I knew best: Sowbhagyavati, delicate, wrapped in a printed sari, her two long plaits tucked behind her, perplexed as she often was by my behavior, so her aunt had once told me.

"She admires you greatly, though," the woman had added. "She knows no one else who reads poetry so well."

We were standing side by side in the SuperBazaar, at the checkout counter. I had smiled in a tight, embarrassed fashion, though I was pleased too. Now the young woman was staring at me. Next to her was Bakshi, cocksure, his cloth cap thrust back on his head.

"Theme of lecture, madam?"

I could tell he was trying to help me on. He knew I wrote poetry and that sometimes my mind did not quite latch onto the particulars of Wordsworth or Arnold, until a line or an image sang out. Clearly today I was in some trouble. Behind him was fierce young Chandrika, her eyes covered by thick spectacles. She was a card-carrying member of the CPM and openly critical of some of my speculations. Yet she was surprisingly sensitive to Matthew Arnold's anguish. She seemed to understand it. Or perhaps it just confirmed her political views on the necessity of change.

In his early twenties, Chandrika's father had been a secretary of Subhas Chandra Bose, and the ideals of using violence to combat violence were quite clear in his daughter's mind. She was contemptuous of what had become of the Gandhians in our lifetime. She observed the way in which petty politicians swarming around Limca Gowda picked up the clothing and overtly abstemious habits of the Gandhians, using it all in public to confound the populace and gain votes.

At Sagar Talkies about a month earlier there had been a documentary to promote good habits in Hyderabad. Little Mother had been keen on going and asked me along. So one evening after a light supper we walked down the road together and sat in the red rexine seats watching the show. Small bits of common sense shot through the script. Little commands peppered it. Do not stand near an exposed light switch during a thunderstorm. Do not pick up a poisonous snake in your bare hands (this always provoked great laughter). Do not drink. Do not try to have more than two children. Do not throw waste into the streets. Do not spit in buses. In the fashion of late eighteenth-century didacticism, each command had a little episode that illustrated the implicit moral. But there was nothing subtle about the film. The maid servant with disheveled hair who plonked herself down near the light switch during a thunderstorm, shuddered terribly as lightning struck. Finally she was permitted to expire. The man who raced imprudently into the busy street to toss out his rubbish got hit in the side by a rickshaw. The youth leaning over to spit in a bus started to choke. And so it went.

At the end of the documentary came a film clip of Gandhi just before the Salt March started, the wind blowing on his taut figure, the sun in his eyes, the specter of the British troops massed against the satyagrahis filling us all, so that the earlier commonsense dicta faded into the sepia of his figure and the frame of our lives seemed momentarily continuous with the past in a longed-for myth. We were magnified in our own eyes and forgot the peeling theater, the crowds leaning forward in their hot seats, the small children chewing toffees.

Then, in a quick cut, came images of Limca Gowda, Chief Minister of Hyderabad, so startling that we held our breath. His large figure was dressed in khadi, and he was standing at the edge of the post office in Hyderabad, or was it by the river? The background was so blurred that it was hard to tell. The wind was in his clothing too. His hands were held aloft. "Father of Hyderabad," shouted some voices, which were picked up and heightened so that the sound track resembled the confusions of a morcha, of the kind where hundreds of peasants were driven in from miles away in the terrible heat of noonday. The promise of a free meal brought them in. Refusal had its costs too. And so it was that Limca's name was chanted at demonstrations or at those special events orchestrated for dignitaries from Delhi.

The following day in class, in a discussion of Romantic myths of the Golden Age I mentioned Limca's public relations film. Chandrika leaned forward and announced in a clear, loud voice that for her study group she was doing an analysis of the Limca film clip.

"He's making myth of himself. You know that, don't you?" she challenged me. "In some way its tied up to all this Wordsworthian stuff you're teaching us, Miss. I'm sure it is."

She had looked tired that particular day. And she needed a response. But all I had said was, "Come let's talk about it sometime?" It was a mild suggestion, intended to let me off the hook and everyone realized it.

Now my own vagueness latched in my mind as I saw her watching me. Was she right? Was there some link I had missed between Limca and the kinds of poetry I loved? I dismissed the thought. I would start from where I was. I would say what I wanted to say, and they would listen me out.

I gripped the edge of the blackboard. I drew a diagram, rather like a conical hat. It was a rough triangle with arrows running from top to bottom and left to right. "World Out There" I put on the right-hand side. "Inner Self" I wrote on the left, and at the top, where the arrows met in a slightly smeared point, I put "Romantic Object." It gave me some pleasure to watch the students bent over their notebooks copying my picture.

I started in a monotone: "Romanticism is the belief in the self, the sense that the object only has value insofar as it is lit by the gaze." This sounded good, almost like a book. There was a small fruit fly bothering me. I flicked it away.

"Now let's bring this a little closer to hand."

To start with I read out the phrases on the diagram. This composed me a little, allowed my voice to reach out.

"This morning on my way to Sona Nivas I passed Optical Palace. I am sure that all of you know that shop. It stands at the corner of Nampally Road. I've seen at least one or two of you take your custom there."

Everyone was listening. I too was waking up. The world was pouring into me. We were coming closer to home. Now the laughter of the painters hanging on the scaffolding outside did not matter so much.

"They have quite a display on the street front, hundreds of spectacles. Some have plastic rims, some metal rims, some bone rims. The lenses are all kinds of colors, pink, purple, blue, green, gray. See how we can transform the world?"

I smiled, relaxing a little. I noticed that Chandrika was frowning at my humor.

"There are literally hundreds of spectacles, and they twist and turn on their little wires catching all that's to be seen, a multitude of images, all fractions of our world: the pavement, the seller of mangoes with his twisted knee, the edge of the Gandhi statue, the poor orange seller, the fat liquor merchant, even the blind beggar who stands there day after day, his back so straight against the sign that reads OPTICAL PALACE, VISION'S GLORY. Remember it?"

I paused. I did not want to lose my listeners. All this was from the world we lived in, and it was quite far from the Wye Valley poem that they were supposed to have read for today. But if I couldn't make a connection what was the point? I continued with the thread of my argument.

"If caught and fixed for an instant, would those hundreds of lenses capture the world? Would they tell the truth about Nampally Road? And how would that truth relate to the 'picture of the mind' the Wye Valley poet talks about? Mr. Wordsworth, remember him? Is there any connection at all?"

Bakshi was stirring in his seat. He started to roll up his shirt sleeves in a slow, lazy fashion.

"Or is there a world, indeed, apart from our seeing it?"

I stopped short. I had to keep them listening.

"Of course, Chandrika, you would argue that was foolish, no? Even a pernicious question? Of course the world exists. The question is, how does it form us? How does history make us?"

Across the open doorway, across the balcony that ran the length of the first floor of Sona Nivas I could make out the shabby tin-roofed buildings of the income tax office, the bolder red-painted walls of the liquor shop, and then the blue gates of the Divine Life Temple, so close that when its loudspeakers were turned on the devotionals drowned out all our voices.

Each year hundreds of devotees came to Hyderabad from as far away as California and Perth. They dressed in thin saffron clothing and sang in the streets, sometimes entering the college to try to gain a few followers. Mostly the students just stared at them or engaged them in chitchat about Capitalism and the Wrongs of Religion. The devotees, often young men and women who had fled their difficult parents and intransigent worlds, smiled docilely and repeated truths about Krishna's love, which coming from their mouths hung like innocent butterflies in our air, weightless, irresolute. Right now none of the devotees were visible, but I could see the queues that had formed outside the income tax office. Its steps rose up in the heat. A sudden reminder of other steps I had just seen. I stared at Bakshi. His uncle was a policeman.

"I am troubled, my friends. There is trouble in our streets. Two days ago some innocent orange sellers were struck on the head as they were trying to organize a peaceful protest against taxes. That too is our world. The world in which we sit trying to read the Wye Valley poem. Trying to bring it closer to home. The orange sellers, the woman raped and beaten."

I stopped. I forced myself to go on. I could feel the old choking sensation coming on me. If I didn't continue I would have lost out, and all my worlds would lie inside me, churning in chaos.

"The use of 'the picture of the mind,' as he calls it so elegantly, is that it clarifies the world. Our world even. And Wordsworth is quite truthful about doubts and dismays, the slow workings of consciousness."

Outside, the sun was getting hotter and we were fanning ourselves with bits of paper. Up on the high gopiram of the temple the sacred lotus shone, its thousand and one petals clearly visible in the cloudless sky. I longed to stop. But I had to make sense, at least to myself. The students were all listening, watching intently as if I were a trickster at a fair who swallows pin and plate and apple and struggles to make them all rise up, whole and clean from her guts. Or will she make a pure new thing, a living dove or a hummingbird from all that stuff?

"Just after this class, if all goes according to plan, we will have a department meeting. At the meeting Professor Saab will ask me to keep notes in triplicate. Why triplicate? It was a practice set in motion by the East India Company. Lest one paper get lost, one important notation perish, each was copied in threes and each copy sent out in a different ship. Why should we do it? Is the question akin to why study Wordsworth in our new India?

"It's a good question. I value Wordsworth for his great privacy of mind and his power. For his illuminations about memory. For his voice so refined that we can listen intently and then say, no our lives are not like that. We live with turmoil and disturbance, with the abuse of law. But as a young man he knew a little about that too. Let me tell you."

I never finished the remark. Ramu ran in through the door. His face shone with sweat. He was shaking with fatigue, with some intense emotion he was struggling to contain.

"Mira, you have to come with me. Dismiss your class now and come."

I did not stop to question him. Something in me was prepared already. I turned back to the students who had half risen.

"There is an emergency. I am terribly sorry. Wordsworth will have to wait. Please read 'Tintern Abbey' over again."

Then I ran along the balcony with Ramu. The leaves of the neem trees that grew in the garden were level with our faces. I saw the small hairs on his forearms. His skin was golden in that gentle light screened through the guava branches that grew in Sarojini Naidu's garden. The heat did not matter anymore. As we hurried down the staircase toward the street I could hear the loudspeaker in the temple cranking up. Soon the devotionals would flood the street.

"Little Mother, she's very ill, but Rani and the apothecary are with her. I promised her I'd tell you. But the Gowliguda affair is more urgent still. We have to rush to the police station now or else they'll finish her off. She's half dead as it is. She's a witness, Mira. She can tell us what really happened."

He gripped my arm and we both raced down Nampally Road.

CHAPTER SIX

RAMEEZA BE

Our running had a life of its own, as if the haste and breathlessness were a world entire. I had felt the same uncertainty in the long air voyages that took me away and brought me back to India when I was a student. Worlds suspended, lives closing up, hanging fire. Now I felt as if I were breaking apart as I ran, and the little splinters hung in the air, in the crows, in the glittering particles of the lotus set atop the temple. Beggars sat hunched over in the courtyard of the temple. They had come from great distances for a handful of grain. Small children clung to their mothers. The heat made my sari stick to my legs, and I had to lift it off my ankles in order to run.

We passed the crossroads by Mirror Mahal, a shop run by a Punjabi salesman. He hung his mirrors out on the pavement and the world shone into them and broke loose at dizzying speed. The catch of my foot soles on the ground was a comfort. I saw a woman cobbler bent over, cutting up small pieces of leather. She had spread a cloth on the pavement, a little to the right of Mirror Mahal. She was so intent on what she was doing that she missed us waving at her. I knew her a little. From time to time she mended my chappals. Ramu did not slow down at all, and I was coughing and gasping for breath before we reached the open space where the Gowliguda police station stood.

When Ramu came to pull me out of Sona Nivas, at first I had no clear idea of where he was taking me. When he told me that Little Mother was terribly ill, my first instinct was to run to her side. But he wouldn't let me. His grip was like iron. And somehow I trusted him. It was like trusting the rough surface of Nampally Road, or the air that sometimes makes you cough as smoke drifts south from the bicycle factories or when tires are burned at night during demonstrations, making the nostrils of those who watch grow puffy and red. But still one goes on breathing, trusting the air.

So I ran with him down the side road, past the New Mysore Cafe and round the railway station, past the sellers of sandalwood and incense, past the young mothers clutching their infants to their swollen breasts. I could hear the rickshaw drivers cry out as we raced past them, I could hear the fishwives and the sellers of vegetables, all the way to the open space where the police station stood.

Already a small crowd had gathered. People stood talking in knots. They were agitated, unresolved about action until a lion of a man tugged off his red shirt, unwrapped his bandana, and with shoulder muscles gleaming above his great chest, raised his arms with a loud martial cry. He was clearly a kabbadi master and proud of his art. He turned his body into a piston, bending forward, exerting huge pressure on the arm muscles. Beside him scores of men and women thrust hard against the main doors of the police station. The wood was old and gave way easily. A stream of people burst in behind the kabbadi master, up the stone steps where two nights earlier the policemen had dragged Rameeza.

Ramu and I got there just in time to see the kabbadi master stride up the steps. It was obvious Ramu knew him, but I did not know from where. He called after him but with the jostle of people all around, the large man did not hear. This time we both entered the building.

The police office had been built by the British in the style of cantonment architecture: stone steps, a gracious verandah, white pillars, and the whole edifice whitewashed to keep the heat at bay. But as we entered, the main room seemed curiously empty. It had a low wooden platform with a large teak table, three chairs behind it all in a row, and on the polished surface a leather-bound book propped open, a steel pen attached to the spine with a bit of string. Two portraits hung above the platform, two visitors from our history: Gandhi drawn in faded brown ink with parted lips, tiny brown spectacles and a bent nose. He held a telephone in his right hand. I noticed the mosquitoes buzzing over the bit of the glass frame where his spectacles were. To the right was a portrait of Nehru, erect, handsome, his cap pointed, polished on his head. His teeth gleamed in the photograph, clearly brushed each morning, an aristocrat lacking a phone line with the future.

Her sari was stiff with blood. I could tell by looking. She lay curled up on the mud floor of the cell just behind the wooden desk. Her face was held up by the mud. In spite of the mosquitoes buzzing over her, both eyes were open. She was breathing in jagged, irregular breaths. I gripped the cell bars and stared and stared at her. I bent forward, and half crouching put my hand through the bars and touched her damp forehead. The hair from her head was plastered in a light mat on her cheeks, held together with blood. It was all dark, the blood, the smear of earth from the cell floor, and the great welts on her face. Her cheekbones were so fine, they might have been composed with clear brush strokes.

There was a commotion just behind. A group of young men struggled with a policeman. They had caught him by surprise.

"Where is she? Where have you taken her?"

I could hear the words shouted out as several policemen came forward from a cubicle at the back of the room. I turned away from Rameeza and noticed the brilliant ribbons, the golden epaulettes stitched to the policeman's uniform. He had an immaculate mustache and a swagger stick under his arm. I watched in a daze as men swarmed over each other, shouting in the corner of the main room and others pounded up the steps, swarming forward. Smoke was everywhere. I started coughing. Someone pushed me aside. Hands tore at the bars. Someone used an iron rod. Finally the padlock gave way and several arms reached in and lifted up Rameeza. I saw her pupils dilate as they carried her out, irises rimmed with night, so black, whole cities might have plunged in them and remained intact, flooded by ruin on the other side of hell. I thought I heard her babbling something, but in that crush of men and women I could not be sure, for I was trying to save myself from being trampled.

To the cries of men and women using milk bottles and soda bottles and bottles filled with kerosene, bearing sticks and stones and bits of lumber in the clear afternoon heat, the police station started burning. It burned very well. Almost as if the old plaster and worn-out teak beams were waiting for an excuse. Toward the end only the metal bars from the cells were left, red hot, bent into S shapes.

"Like infernal serpents," Ramu told me later.

A cur dog was found in the ashes, roasted alive. Its toenails were intact, miraculously saved by the bricks that had fallen over its legs, pinning it down in the blaze. Of the two portraits, nothing was left, not even the metal frames.

Now Rameeza's story spread through Hyderabad like smoke from the burning police station. A young woman had come in from the mountains with her husband. They had gone to see the celebrated *Isak Katha* at Sagar Talkies. It was late at night. Walking back to the home of relatives, along the deserted road in Gowliguda, they fell prey to a horde of drunken policemen. Rameeza was gang raped. Her husband had his brains beaten out. His body was recovered from a well behind the police station. Swollen, the eyes puffed out, it was identified by his brother, a lorry driver in Hyderabad. Now the police station was burning, iron bars and all, a quick, sudden revenge.

By the time the hundreds of reserve police and the gangs of Ever Ready men arrived on the scene, there was nothing much to do except watch the police station burn. Rameeza had been carried away to a safe house, and most of the people had dispersed. Those who remained, throwing bricks and bottles at the handful of policemen on duty, were quickly arrested and carted off in the black vans.

The Chief Minister's birthday was coming closer and the disruption had to be "contained." That was the verb used in the *Deccan Herald* and announced on the radio news. A search was on for the enemies of the law and for the woman Rameeza, source of the turbulence. Rewards were announced for finding her. Five noble policemen suffered head injuries, the news said, though no one was seriously hurt. The Ever Ready jingle

> Ticktock ticktock
> Ever Ready Ever Ready
> EverReady Battery -o

was played louder than ever before. There were several items of news on All-India Radio about encounters with armed students, members of the Naxalite groups in the hills north of the city. The next day dozens of student leaders, workers, and a handful of intellectuals who were thought to be subversives were rounded up and arrested. They were to be held in "protective detention," it was said, until the Chief Minister's birthday was over. No one knew where Ramu was. It was not clear if he was among those who had been arrested.

Sitting by Little Mother's side as she lay on her sick bed, I listened carefully to the radio announcements. The broadcasts said large forces of reserve police were being sent to Hyderabad by the central government. I turned the radio off and listened to the sounds from the window. The window was closed tight on the apothecary's advice, lest the night air harm Durgabai. I could hear very little.

CHAPTER SEVEN

HER FEVER

Little Mother was so pale, it was as if her sheets had taken hold of her and drawn her into them, a burial in cotton.

All the color had drained out of her face. Though she burned with a high fever, her hands and feet felt like blocks of ice. A day and a half after the burning of the police station she was delirious. She twisted and turned in her bed, chattering about her mother. She was so cold that her fingernails danced on the bedsheets and she clenched her hands together when she was strong enough. When she wasn't I held her palms in both of mine, rubbing hard so that some life would return to her.

Broken syllables dashed from her mouth. I thought I heard bits and pieces of languages, all the tongues it seemed the world had ever held. At odd moments vowels flashed by me. They were so pure they could only have been released by intense pain, or that ecstasy most of us know just once or twice in a lifetime.

Sometimes she was intelligible. She cried out loud about the boy with his brain chewed up by maggots, about her dead husband. Sometimes she seemed to be calling her son Siddharth, crying out as if her voice could reach into the shabby room above the pawnshop five thousand miles away.

Her body was drenched in sweat. The lamplight shone into her hair as it lay tangled on the pillow, a great mass of darkness shot through with silver. The length of jasmine rope Rani had given her that morning lay suppurating, petals sickly with sweat. I tried to free it from her head but a single knot of bloom resisted, embedded in a ball of hair. I searched for the scissors to cut it free, but then bent and smoothed the tangle under the pillow as she lay there, her mouth barely trembling, utterly spent.

On the apothecary's advice we decided to send for Ranga Reddy, the famous physician. Ranga Reddy had a hard time getting to us. The road from his palatial office was blocked by the barricades. There were gangs of armed men roaming the streets, and women and children were warned to stay indoors. At any moment a curfew would be announced.

Ranga Reddy adjusted his spectacles and motioned to his servant boy to set his bag on the table by the mirror. He peered down at Durgabai. He did not like what he saw. He had brought various pills with him, each dose wrapped up in white paper. He laid these out on the dressing table with strict instructions as to how they were to be doled out. The apothecary was fascinated and watched with great care. His suggestion that leeches be administered to Little Mother was dismissed with contempt by the doctor. He brushed the apothecary away with distaste. The little man was quite mortified and whispered his humiliation to Rani in the kitchen, in between great gulps of tea he gave himself as a prophylactic lest the fever pass to him. Each night either Rani or I slept in her room so that Little Mother would never be alone.

Months later she told me her dreams. It was as if the unrest that was creeping through the city had entered her feverish soul. In a recurrent dream she found herself running and running as hard as she could down Nampally Road.

"Child, I don't even know what became of my sari, so hard I ran." Why was she running? I asked her. She had no idea. "It may have just been delirium, but I don't think it was just that."

As I listened to her speak, I felt that our thoughts were crossing each other like two tracks that run parallel and at some unseen point in the desert, precisely where the mirage rises, converging in a heat that disrupts all vision. They have a power of feverish motion, these dreams of ours, they trap us, yet cut us free from the pots and pans and syringes of our daily lives.

Those days were hard. I thought constantly of the burning of the police station and the terror that had befallen Rameeza. I had come so close to her, yet knew so little. I longed to search her out. Yet I was bound here, to Little Mother who clearly needed me. In her sickness I found an image of our lives. The fever that rose, swelling her hands and feet and face, was part of the same fever that was tearing apart the city.

Classes were cancelled at Sona Nivas. Curfew was forced. In order to get vegetables Rani had to wake up very early and run to the market. Sagar Talkies cancelled their normal evening shows, and the street hung curiously silent. It was eerie listening to the street and not catching the laughter and loud shouts, the sounds of rickshaws and bullock carts grinding forward, the hooting of taxis. The only real sound was that of lorries bearing cardboard archways and cut tendrils of the palmyra, bits and pieces of prefabricated platform, chairs and loudspeakers to the Public Gardens where Limca Gowda's birthday was to be celebrated in a few days.

Durgabai was as weak as a baby, and I spent a great deal of time with her indoors. The uncertainty in the air invaded me. I seemed to myself to be a small stick insect suspended on a surface of clear ice, ignorant of whether what held me up might melt. Down below and all around I could see the ordinary world, but nothing touched me. We were living our lives out second by second. Even our gestures seemed frozen. There was nothing but to wait it out.

As a discipline I set to observing the colors of bee wings as they hovered over the jasmine bush. I tried to recall the lines made by moss on the stones in the graveyard outside my window. Twice I tried to call Ramu's home, but the lines were out of order. I told myself what in any case was forced on me, that it would be the better part of wisdom to wait for him to call. Waiting did not become me. I grew tense and harried, and sometimes the slightest sound at the gateway made me start. I had grown frightened, dependent, as if the chaos that was unleashed in the city had robbed me of my nerve. I was waiting for Little Mother to recover. I was waiting for Ramu to call me.

One night when it was hotter than usual, I heard Little Mother stir. I followed her, anxious not to disturb her privacy. I had been sitting reading in an alcove in the drawing room, next to the Ganapati statue. Rani was nowhere to be seen. It must have been close to eleven at night. Little Mother was stronger now, able to walk around, feed herself, drink the doses of glucose water the doctor had prescribed.

In the moonlight that flooded in through the windows, she found her way to the kitchen. I was worried that she might be sleepwalking, and putting aside the book I was reading, a copy of Sankara's *Vivekachudamani* that Swami Chari had recommended to me, I crept in after her. I found her pale but utterly lucid, standing at the kitchen stove. There was a little light coming in from the street lamps. The woodburning stove that was built onto the small platform jutting out of the wall showed two dark holes. Overhead pots hung low in their cradles of string and rope. She was bent over the stove stirring a pot of water with dal in it. I could see that she had added turmeric and a dash of salt, the simplest possible accompaniment for a meal.

"You found me out then?" Her voice cut me to the quick. I felt ashamed for having followed her. "No need to explain. I just wanted to move about a bit and make myself useful. What a mess the kitchen is. And where is Rani?"

"She might be at Laura's. Do you want me to call her?"

She brushed off the question.

"Here, get this off the stove, quick."

A slow smoke was pouring out of the stove. The wood was damp, or perhaps she hadn't rubbed the sticks together to make them bristle with heat before lighting them. She was worn out and the smoke was in her eyes. I settled her on the stool by the window and pulled out some of the half-burnt wood. There was a film of moisture at the end. I looked around for some dry wood to use. If there was none I would prime the kerosene stove. We had run out of gas, and the cylinders were impossible to replace. They had to be driven in from fifteen miles away and all the roads were closed. I knew of poor women in the old city who had to walk miles in the darkness, before the curfew hours, to search for firewood.

Chandrika had visited one morning and told me of their plight. In sharp, bitter detail she described the difficulties of ordinary life under the curfew. I introduced her to Little Mother, who was able to sit up by that time. Chandrika was convinced that the capitalist systems were falling apart, that Hyderabad was the flashpoint for revolution. But even she could acknowledge the power of Limca Gowda's troops.

"But look how the police station was burned down," she argued. "It was an act of spontaneous rage. On the part of the people. The question now is, how are we going to channel the rage, what are we to do with it? We must work forward."

"Is it true that something will happen on the maidan during the birthday celebrations?"

Chandrika had refused to be drawn out. She stood up straightening her long skirts, adjusting her spectacles on her nose. I offered her a volume of Sartre's essays I had with me. I thought she might enjoy them. She had left clutching the book under her arm. It was the last I saw of her. She was barely eighteen years old.

Now Little Mother, sitting quite erect on the stool, looked at me quizzically.

"Have you heard from your student again, that young woman, Chandrika? She was so earnest. I wished to calm her, but she understood things that are difficult really. And where is Ramu these days? "

I turned to her unhappily.

"I have no idea where Ramu is. But I'm sure he'll come soon."

I stumbled on, holding the pot of dal in my hands.

"I'm afraid things are going to come down very hard on us in Hyderabad. I just feel that." She was listening intently now.

"I had a dream last night. I was clutching the edge of a great pyramid made of bricks. The bricks were all jagged, all askew as if the pyramid were immensely old, or had been made by an unskilled laborer. But the bricks were not really bricks. I realized this as I held on for dear life. There was black water rushing all around me, and the water was climbing higher and higher. The bricks were alive. They were made of flesh. Human flesh. And they had voices that cried out in a tumult of tongues. As the water rose bit by bit, I struggled to climb higher. And far away as the eye could see was water, black water. Until to the right, all of a sudden I saw a small fire, rocking in that water. And then the fire grew and it invaded the water, and took dominion over it, and approached the pyramid where I still clung with all those crying voices of flesh. I couldn't bear it. I tried to wake up."

I was trembling now, and she rose to try to get me to put down the pot of dal lest I drop it on myself or smash the pot. Already some of the water with the reddish lentil in it had trickled onto the floor.

"You think seeing that poor raped woman has something to do with the dream?"

I was grateful for her wisdom.

"The water was just the color of her eyes as I looked in through the bars."

We gazed at each other in silence. On the road outside, the distant rumble of traffic was audible, then a sharp crack as if a gunshot had sounded. The high-pitched crying of voices was borne to us on the wind from the far-off rubber factory. It was a tumult of voices mixed with wind.

And we just sat there in the half darkness, two women with the pot of dal bubbling on the stove, listening to the cries of men and women, rustling leaves, electric cicadas, fireflies, slow worms, all the small creatures of the earth mixed together. The city we inhabited was driven into unrest, yet the natural darkness comforted, the indigo of night lining high clouds, a lemon colored moon.

She was comfortable on the stool, lulling herself, crooning almost as if she were on the brink of singing a lullaby.

"Look at this branch, child."

Through the barred window she pulled in a thick-leaved branch of the peepul tree. The leaves were glossy, vital, each parting from the central stalk into its own particular life. A green livelihood, a knowledge in a time of difficulty.

"Here, touch the leaves. Years ago when Mother was contructing the house, I must have been ten or eleven then, I imagined Sri Krishna tumbling down the branches in sheer sport. It was all so open here. No Sagar Talkies. No Laura's flat. Not even Feroze Gandhi Park where the Parsis let their chickens run loose. It was all rough pastureland . And all around us were huge cuts in the red earth as the men dug and dug and drew up great stone blocks for the foundations and set up the main doorway, covering it each night with a few scattered grains of rice so the spirits would rest. The outer gate has always held firm. A drummer sat up there for my wedding. Poor man, he fell off, I think."

She wiped her eyes with the edge of her sari, then moved to stir the dal. Our modest scheme of cooking comforted us both. She coughed a little, then shifted the pot to the side of the stove, its blackened base transferring itself to her, soot filming her palms like a second skin, so fine that the tiny markings on her upturned palms were visible. She was washing her hands now.

"Did your mother cook?"

"A little now and then. A great deal on feast days. She had her special dishes though. Srikhand so fragrant you thought your whole mouth was melting. 'A feast for the apsaras,' Father would call it. Threads of saffron hung on the surface of the delicate mounds of white. She was pleased when he said that."

We moved away from the kitchen as the sounds of unrest mixed with the wind and something acrid that might have been tear gas wafted in through the kitchen window. In that brief span of moonlight before the city convulsed, we sat side by side talking. Her voice was cool, lyrical, as if her sickness, the frenzy of my dreams, or the violence around us had never been. Or as if she had within her a power of thought so deep she could let it all be, all at once, the terror and the poise, the voices wafting in the moonlight and the tear gas pouring in acrid, diluted puffs through the kitchen window. She was thinking of her mother. As if she sensed the loneliness in me, she wanted me to know her mother.

"She always used to wear a blue sari. During that whole year of house building she wore blue. Watching her day after day the labor settled into the mind, the rhythmic motion of bricks being picked up and laid on the foundation, pickaxes flashing in the air as more earth was dug, a series so compelling that time was held in balance. It seemed as if nothing could hurt us. She had her black umbrella and stood in the unfinished courtyard, just there, directing the work. Each night by the light of the oil lamp I can still see the shadow of her shoulders and neck on the wall as she pored over the accounts given her by the contracters, the suppliers of stone and wood. Slowly, with great care, she added up the sums of money, subtracting them from the total allotted for that span of work. Father was never there. He was always travelling in Nagpur to see to the orange groves, or he was away at the Nizam's palace."

She paused heavily. She seemed a little short of breath.

"I used to jump on the paving stones, one by one as they laid them flat. I'd jump over and over the stones or even the string they stretched in squares to mark out the plan for the courtyard. All the time mother was watching me through the corner of her eye."

So I sat listening to Little Mother's story, the world maintained in a poise made by her voice. We had a very simple meal that night, our chairs drawn up to the table's edge so that each of us could see the moon as it slipped in and out of the clouds and hung over the tulasi leaves. They shimmered as water might when the scales of fishes strike it. In moonlight the courtyard had a light lavender tint and a few fireflies clustered in the orange bush making balls of hanging flame. I kept watching for a dark shadow, such as Rani might throw if she were creeping back home, but there was no sign of her.

I helped Little Mother stack the plates back in the kitchen sink and then hooked down the shutter by the peepul tree in case there was rain that night. She was tired now and I urged her to prepare for bed, but neither of us wanted to break up the evening that had started so fortuitously. So I sat at the edge of the bed in Little Mother's bedroom. She was searching through a pile of papers on her desk.

I watched her in the long mirror on her dressing table. The table held several objects that were dear to her. There was a small tin with a mango leaf painted on the lid. It held her pins. Then there was an old bone comb and a hairnet left loosely at the side. Each object was reflected in the mirror. The mirror was quite old and the silver was coming apart, revealing the black paint at the back, but in the middle distance was a tall woman, her large shoulders and back dipping into the pallor of the wall behind. I straightened up. The image was disconcerting. I craned my neck to look at her. Little Mother was coming toward me.

"Sit, sit," she beckoned.

I waited for her, as she sat quite straight at the edge of the chair and drew out her long hair. I passed her the comb. As she pulled out the hairpins I heard the wind battering the trees outside. A single branch scraped at the shutters on the street side of her bedroom. Everything else was quiet. Then the rain started.

She moved her chair closer to the dressing table so that she could rest her feet on the lowest drawer. She turned to me. I was seated on her bed, a pillow behind my back. As she spoke, her voice mingled with the sounds of the rain on the roof and the branches, on the soil, the asphalt, the garbage mound outside. The disturbances in the city seemed very far away.

"It was a night rather like this. Rain on the trees. This time of year too. We were sitting in the drawing room, all of us, when Savitribai came in."

She was referring to her older sister, now living in Pune.

"She's five years older than I am. Her face was trembling. It was very odd. Not her hands, but her face. Shaking with great emotion. Savitribai was always so controlled."

Little Mother held up her two hands to the mirror, watching the image they made. She was quite intent, holding them apart, then moving the fingers in a gesture so quick it seemed as if a dancer had made them, the half-finished mudra cut by an instant of hesitation, the sign of the lotus or the bee in flight trapped in incompletion as the audience hung on her grace, waiting. She sighed. She closed her palms together and folded them in her lap.

"I made her sit down. And what a tale it was, child."

I closed my eyes to listen better. I loved her voice. It wove the world together. It made a past. Listening to her, I lost the bitter sense I often had of being evicted, of being thrust out of a place in which lives had meanings and stories accreted and grew. The present was flat and sharp and broken into pieces. There was tear gas in the present and a woman's terrible cry still hovering over a burnt out police station.

"I told you she was trembling. So I made her sit down. I put out my hands and touched her hair. It was all wet with sweat. Her pupils were dilated with exhaustion. She had been away in the Nizam's palace for a whole day and a half, delivering his fourth wife's baby."

I sat up with a start. I stared at her. For a few moments I had fused her voice with the quivering face of Rameeza Be. Over and over in my mind I had pondered that meeting, those great eyes blackened with despair, with incomprehension.

"It was a son, almost born dead. The cord was noosed around its throat. It was the most difficult labor Savitribai had seen.

"She rubbed the woman with hot oil, applied cold poultices to her body, then finally packed her hips and torso in ice. It was the only way to stop the bleeding.

"She picked up the tiny baby in her arms. It was all blue, black-blue really, a kind of indigo. Lord Krishna's color."

She smiled at me, crinkling up her eyes. She was taking pleasure now in her own story, weaving it in and out of deep memory.

"The tiny mouth was moist, all shut. So she opened it with her little finger and poured in breath from her own lungs, until it started breathing better. And all the while the Nizam, not as mad as you think, though indeed he had that reputation, paced outside the room. His jewelled heels made such a clatter on the marble.

"Poor Savitribai, she wanted terribly to save the child. It was a life. God knows what would have happened to all of us if that child had died. He's a businessman now in Australia. Import-export business, Raghavan told me. Air conditioners, I think. He did the antique business before, exporting valuables to Austria and the United States. He wanted to sell off some of the priceless glassware, chandeliers, and crystal from the palace before the government seized all the property.

"When the baby was breathing properly, the Nizam summoned her in. Fatima, the fourth wife, the one who had just given birth, was sleeping quietly on her tiger skins. Quite unhygienic, but he insisted on it. So Savitribai walked in, just as she was, sari still damp with patches of blood and mucus. She walked into the imperial throne room. I remember her telling me later that there were electric lights hidden in the marble trellis work and bidri vases of the most intricate designs, large as a small calf. The vases were filled with grain for the birds. You've heard of the birds, haven't you? He would let them out each night, and they made a most terrible mess in the throne room, flapping wings, shedding feathers, feeding, and excreting all at once while the emperor, unable to bear his own emotions, would race up and down amid them. Having fun. Having fun! They had to wash out the room each time the birds had left. It took twenty courtiers to catch them and shut them in their cages again.

"Well, this time there were no birds in sight. Just the old man reasonably sober, sitting cross-legged on the throne. He called her to come all the way and showered her with a handful of gold. Gold sovereigns, the kind one doesn't see anymore. Poor Savitri scooped them up, very nervous now. The Nizam was not known for his moderation.

"Wanting to say 'I did my duty,' or something of the sort, she just stuttered. The exhaustion was starting to catch up with her. After all, the labor had gone on for a day and a half. Dry labor too, for Fatima's waters had burst as she lay on the tiger skins being fanned by her attendants. Years later Fatima went crazy. She had to be confined to a dark chamber. It was said she turned quite violent. Tore up all the furnishings in her bedroom, tiger skins as well. By that time of course the emperor was far gone himself.

"So there was Savitri, her clothes all streaked with bloodstains clutching the gold coins in her right hand and making her way, bit by bit, backward over the carpets, hoping to god she wouldn't trip over a vase filled with bird seed. She could feel all the courtiers staring at her.

"Our family was held in high esteem ever after, though Father could never stand that man's atrocities. He used to make his servants leap into pools of boiling water to retrieve pearls that he tossed in. Anyone who even faltered was half flayed, so bad the floggings were. In any case, if you weren't quick enough the boiling water would do you in."

She held her breath at the cruelty she recounted, then turned to a tale a little closer at hand.

"Poor old Pithulbhai, the apothecary's maternal uncle. He was forced by the Nizam's vizier to give up his peacock gardens, all for a mere pittance, a handful of turmeric. The old man took it. It was all the dowry he had for his harelipped daughter. She never married of course. She must be very old now, but I think she used to sweep out the Gowliguda police station and take water to the few prisoners there. Some say she works as a midwife too, helping with particularly difficult labors."

"Do you know where the old woman is now?"

"Didn't the apothecary say she lives near King Koti? In those small tin-roofed shacks there? Why do you ask?"

I didn't want to reply. I did not know how to pull it all out of me from where it lay coiled up, a dark incipient life. How Ramu had taken me to the police station. How I had seen Rameeza. How just as the fire blazed I had heard someone whispering that Rameeza would be taken care of in Pithulbhai's daughter's house. If Little Mother hadn't been so ill at the time I would have told her about it all.

"I just wondered. You know that poor woman Rameeza Be. Perhaps Pithulbhai's daughter knows her. Knows where she is."

I had just composed the words of a response in my mind, when something I sensed in her tone stopped me. She was still very frail. I did not want to drag her into the turbulence of the world. I watched her closely. Little Mother's hair was all loose and hung over her shoulders. She still held the bone comb in her right hand. Now she looked at it quizzically.

"This was Savitribai's."

I got up to secure the shutters. As I opened the window to get the latch just right, the rising wind caught me by surprise. It was utterly dark. The street lights had blown out. I could smell the rainwater on the damp earth.

She was speaking now, seated so still that she might have been a stone sculpture. She spoke to no one in particular, or, perhaps she spoke to herself, and my being there helped her do so.

"Sometimes I remember so much that I don't know what to do with my life anymore. And don't know who I am. What am I, child, when I don't do my work? Who am I, Mira?"

She tapped the corner of the dressing table, unsettling a fine mixture of face powder and dust.

"I'm thinking of that night just before Savitribai came home, trembling like she did. Father was not with us. He was all alone on the train to Nagpur. Called away. Some trouble on his property. Someone should have accompanied him, but the summons came about Fatima bleeding, and I thought that with Savitribai gone to the palace someone should stay at home.

"It was raining lightly. I was very lonely. I walked out on the roof. I stood under the cover of the peepul branches. The whole city of Hyderabad lay before me. The lights along the river were a string of jewels, and the small fires from the villages north of us still burned. I could see some pleasure boats from the palace moving on the river. The Nizam used to set them afloat on the river, several boats at a time filled with musicians. He always sat in the boat with the blind santur player, the man from Kashmir. Then all the boats vanished. There was just the black river."

She held her wrist with thumb and forefinger, as if feeling for the pulse.

"Must have been a grove of trees shutting them from my sight, or a bend in the river. But in sudden fear my mind moved to Father. I felt the jolting of the train as if I were on it. He was dead already by that time. Slumped over on his seat, that's how they found him. Massive cardiac arrest. Of course I didn't know. I just imagined his death. I was all alone then. I hadn't yet met my husband, you know."

She looked at me as if she saw them both, her father and husband, in the dimness that entered the room. The voltage had fallen and I could hardly see her.

CHAPTER EIGHT

A DARK ROOM

The next morning we woke up very early. The rain had stopped, but it was windy and still threatening. I had slept through the night, untroubled by dreams, but had a curious sense of dislocation when I woke up. Where was I? I thought I knew perfectly well where I was, but there was discomfort in that knowledge, as if with a single false move the world would pool back into the abyss of the mind. I walked out into the courtyard and saw that sparrows had filled the cariapatta bush. Hundreds of feathered bodies weighed down the tender green leaves. The birds were squabbling. As I approached the bush, the central branch bent lower and then trembled as the birds took fright and fled.

"Ah, so there you are!"

Rani appeared out of nowhere. She pointed toward the dining room. Little Mother was awake, and a pot of tea was ready on the table. But instead of drinking her tea she was trying to get the radio to work. The batteries were half dead, and the old box had to be coaxed before any sounds would come out of it. But Rani had more to say.

"Laura's packing up, amma."

"Packing?"

"She feels it's time to leave. Mimi has sent her a ticket. Too much disruption here, Laura says. And Henry's beating her up."

Rani stood with her hands on her hips, quite firm. She did not let on that Laura Ribaldo had promised to invite her to Calgary once she was firmly settled there.

"Look." She pointed over her shoulder to me. I walked to the edge of the courtyard and peered up. There was Laura in her black dress, kneeling by the empty kerosene container they had set out to catch rainwater. She had an open suitcase by her, and she was flinging in cloves, cinnamon, bits of artsilk, enamel pots, an old saucer, joss sticks to burn in front of the icon she had already lifted from the hook in the bedroom and laid out tenderly in the sunlight. I caught my breath. She was packing up her whole world to carry away. I called out to her. She glanced in my direction, half shamefully. There were tears in her eyes. I pretended not to notice what she was doing.

"Little Mother is a lot better," I called out. "She sends her greetings."

"What's that?"

I didn't have time to reply for the radio had started working with a loud blare. I walked indoors, sat at the table, cradling my hot tea and listening with thousands of others all over the city to the voice of Sujit Sen, special broadcaster.

In his deep, clipped voice, well trained by the BBC Overseas Service people he announced the good news. By special decree of the Chief Minister the curfew had been lifted. The strike and the subsequent shooting in the rubber factory were relegated to a brief aside. Order was restored. That was the main theme. There were grand festivities afoot in the city. Now we were just twenty-four hours away from the birthday celebrations. In his well-known narrative style Sujit Sen described the great platforms and archways that were being raised at the outskirts of the Public

Gardens for the pageant. He mentioned the thousands of peasants who were being transported in lorries from the countryside to add their voices to those of the citizens of Hyderabad. Limca Gowda was to be proclaimed the great leader.

"It is a historic moment," the broadcaster noted, a slight catch in his voice.

"There is no doubt that all troublesome elements will be subdued. A new world will arise."

As his voice subsided, loud and clear came the Ever Ready jingle.

> Come and buy Ever Ready
> Battery,
> EverReady battery -o

"The sales of EverReady Batteries have risen in the past year," a woman's voice began, but she was cut off by a high-pitched wailing sound. A special dispatch was announced. Five ringleaders of a conspiracy had been arrested near King Koti. They were carrying arms hidden in their dhotis. It was suspected that the arms had been smuggled in by terrorists in the north.

"Special vigilance is needed," the voice informed the citizens. Rewards were offered for the capture of suspicious people. The radio broadcast was worrisome. The official word was out, and soon the streets would be filled with plainclothesmen. When Ramu arrived a few hours later looking worn out and sleepless, I was so relieved. I slipped my hand into his and drew him into the courtyard. There was a joyful hubbub on the streets. The barber flung his windows open, the bicycle boys giggled at the apothecary, schoolchildren tossed orange pips in the air. I could see a kite in a brilliant saffron color flying over the tamarind trees in the abandoned graveyard. I saw it catch Ramu's eye. It seemed that nothing could stop that kite as it climbed higher and higher into the sky, its tail with long strips of white paper mooring it in the sunlight. I imagined a small child clambering over the gravestones holding the string. Suddenly the kite caught in a tree branch. It hung in the air for an instant, then fell sharply.

Abruptly Ramu got up. I could tell from the pressure on my hand where he still held it that he was very tense.

"Come, we have so little time."

I held onto his arm but did not move. I wanted to stand in the sunlight with him a little, rejoice in the air and the sky. I wanted to take him to Little Mother, perhaps make some coffee so that we could sip it gently, seated in the courtyard. But something was wound up so tightly within him.

"Mira, please."

I followed him out of the courtyard onto the street. Behind us I heard Rani call out, but I ignored her. The street was crowded now. There was rejoicing in the air. At the New Mysore Cafe, Bolaram was passing out bits of ladu and barfi. But we took the other road, the one to King Koti.

It was darker here, as if the sky had worn itself thin in patches and the blue had given way under the pressure of an older turbulence, revealing a darkness that bit into the trees and soldered the dust to our skins. We sat in an autorickshaw, an ancient three-wheeler with a chug-chug motor that drove at breakneck speed past the high walls of the old abandoned houses, toward a stubble field packed with tiny shanties. Soon we were in front of a whole shanty town built of one- or two-room huts, mud floors, roofs of corrugated iron, and, if the occupant was lucky, a minute courtyard. There were open gutters filled with water. Small children squatted there, throwing in pebbles or pissing. We seemed strange in our town garments, in this other city, set within the walls of Hyderabad. Someone cried out. It was a man's voice. Looking for Pithulbhai's daugher, Ramu replied to the unseen auditor.

"Tell her it's a friend."

Someone peered out from behind a wall. Then a figure appeared, waving at Ramu. It was the great-chested muscleman, the kabbadi master I had glimpsed at the police station. He sported a huge mustache, and a red bandana was wrapped around his head.

Our guide led us past mud walls that stood at sharp angles to each other, so that it was impossible to imagine a passage between them. But suddenly, almost when I felt the mud would strike me in the eyes, a small passage appeared and we passed through, edging our bodies sideways, stepping carefully over a thin stream of water. It was yellow like sulphur or urine. A window opened behind and an old wrinkled face appeared, cloth pulled over head and eyes. Suddenly I was frightened. Where had I seen that face before? In a dream? I thought I heard a creature snapping behind us.

"It's only a mongoose," Ramu reassured me.

The man pulled us into a doorway. He had to stoop almost double to enter. He bent his immense weight of rib cage and chest over the tightly knotted dhoti, so that his fitted shirt almost stretched to the breaking point. I do not know how he made it inside. Even I had to crouch down and push myself forward with my hands.

Inside it was cool and dark and wet. An old woman crouched by a pot stirring something. She gestured to us and we squatted on the ground. She rose slowly and approached us, her creased skin making furrows in her face. At her waist a cloth was bound and knotted into a small pouch. It stirred as if something thick were pouring through it.

She came so close to me that her nose scraped mine. I smelled the pungent herbs she was boiling in the pot. Her eyes were hooded by great hanging lids, so that only a fraction of the pupils showed through. Suddenly I felt my fears lift. She pointed to her waist, motioning me. I put out my hand and touched the moving thing she had put there.

She opened it up with great care, and a medium-sized snake uncoiled in a stream of black light. The diamond patterns on its scales caught the glare from the high window. The dazzling snake scales made the small hut clench itself, then burst loose so that even the tin roof where the heat was concentrated seemed higher now, less oppressive. She laughed, displaying her mouth with two jagged teeth.

"Maitreyiamma keeps snakes. Their poison sacks are removed." The kabbadi man was looking at Ramu, but I felt he was speaking to me. "She learned the trick of extracting poison when the family fell on hard times. She carries the water pot to the prisoners at Gowliguda."

Maitreyi put her old hand over the snake and calmed it for an instant, shutting the light from its eyes. Hidden from our gaze the creature subsided. Quickly she pulled the cloth over it.

"She wants to know why you wish to see Rameeza."

He was speaking to Ramu. How had he known we had come to see Rameeza? But then why else would we be here?

"I want to talk to her. I saw her in the police station. How is she?"

"She has no fever now, if that's what you mean."

The old woman snapped at me in her thin voice, "No fever at all. My herbs cured her. Here, come here."

I could not tell if she wanted me to walk with her or was calling someone else into the room. A torn curtain was nailed to a side of the wall, and it moved a little as if a slight wind had entered the room. Then a small hand pulled it up until only a triangle hung between us and the chamber on the other side. I saw a figure, still in an old red sari, lying on a rope bed. Her hands were sore with whatever had hurt her. But the welt on her cheek had subsided, and the blood that had clotted from her wounds had been washed away. Obviously, though, it was difficult for her to move.

When she saw us she raised herself on an elbow and tried to draw her knees into a sitting position. I could not take my eyes off her. I felt her wounds were calling me, crying out in almost inaudible tongues. Her suffering had a language we did not yet understand. My hand tingled as if I still felt the face I had touched through the prison bars. I knelt by her and saw that her eyes were cooler now but maintained that terrible darkness.

She would not speak to us. I think she could not speak to us. She made little whispers and short cries as if she had come from another country and the words we spoke, or even our manner of making them, the physicality of sounds that passed through our lips, meant little to her. Sometimes she pointed to her thin belly covered over with the old red cloth, sometimes to her back, which was badly bruised. All the while the old woman was busy with her pots but clearly watchful.

Ramu and I crouched on the floor by the rope bed, listening to Rameeza. I did not say very much. I just wanted to look at her, feel those eyes again. I wanted to understand her pain. Perhaps it would help us all move forward. Ramu, though, was talking to her, slowly, gently. Speaking political words about his party and about how those who had raped her would be brought to justice. He told her that the people would rise up again. That she would be avenged. I saw her listening. I knew that she must have understood something. But there was no visible sign. Only her right hand, wrapped up in a cloth so that the skin would heal more quickly, twitched suddenly. Her body was like a lovely tree, a guava with its pale skin, filled with angry wounds. A small shake, a twitch, a whisper, a cry that came out of her throat, that was all.

As we sat there in the darkness listening to the rain on the tin roof sounding like piled sand crashing against the delicate walls of a shell, I sensed that she was struggling with something or someone inside her. Over and over this thing pounded at her from the inside and threatened to swallow her back into the silence from which her cries and whispers saved her. All her energy was drained in the struggle. And she did not trust words. I could tell that. Nor could one touch her easily, so wounded and torn was her body that touch must surely have been a source of fear.

The old woman, after watching us for a few minutes, hobbled back into the other room and busied herself. The kabbadi man, without saying a word, walked out. I felt he would be watching us, though, from the other room, or even from the dark passageway. Rameeza motioned with her free hand.

"I think she wants to write something."

"I have some paper, here."

Pleased to be doing something, I picked up a small pad of lined paper I always carried with me. The leaves stuck together and I pried them apart, blowing on them to dry out the damp.

Ramu had a small blue pencil in his shirt pocket. He gave it to me and I held both out to Rameeza.

She tried to push herself up, and I moved closer to her and arranged the old sheet on which she was lying so that it made a small mound on which she could rest her back. She bent her head, and her fine black hair fell over her face. Her hair had been cut short by the old woman. I think there had been too much blood and dirt caught in it. Ramu told me later that her hair had been singed by the fire in the police station and the ends were still smouldering when she was lifted to safety.

I set the pad of paper and pencil beside her. I knew she wanted to pick up the pencil, but it was hard for her. She tried again. The rain grew softer, as if a small wind had pushed the clouds away from us. I heard the mongoose scratching in the room outside. It seemed to live quite peaceably with Maitreyi's snake.

She picked up the pencil in her fist, a woman unused to writing. But it wasn't just that. The skin had come off on the insides of her fingers, and a fist was better. The pad lay on the wooden plank on the bedside. She made a mark running up and down, a line that was jagged as it ran. Then another at an angle to it. Was she trying to write a letter? But it did not look like a letter of the alphabet. It had none of the small curlicues, none of the curving marks that the alphabet required.

Ramu was staring at the two jagged lines and the point at which they met. Rameeza made a third line that closed up the other two into a triangle. Now she was making rough oblong shapes, rectangles, all higgledy-piggledy filling in the triangle. Some of the rectangles were balanced on neighboring rectangles, others filled up the space and left no room, so that the bricks or stones or whatever it was that was pouring from her head crowded into the small space she had marked out with her three lines.

I held my breath. I shut my eyes, not daring to look. She was drawing the great pyramid with stones of flesh that I had seen in my dreams. The stones with water rushing under them, where I had hung. The stones with voices. I was so close to her now that I felt I was writing with her hand, that her hand was my hand writing.

"Look, she's drawing the cell. It's the police station," Ramu whispered. "She's showing us where she was raped."

But suddenly, at the sound of his voice, she stopped and dropped the pencil, as if the spirit had fled.

"No, Ramu, it was something else."

I picked up the pencil and handed it to Rameeza, but she turned her face away, almost as if she were ashamed of the outburst of drawing.

"Can I look at it?"

She nodded. I picked up the small scrap of paper and noticed the pressure marks from her wrist, the small stain of sweat or blood. I saw the way in which the childish pyramid had bricks tumbling out of it, hardly held together. Some bricks had X marks on them, crossings-out that she had done at a furious pace. She was sobbing now, her hair all tangled in her face. Carefully trying to make my flesh as light as air, I bent over and cradled her head in my arms. I could feel her weep now, weep and weep for all the terror that was in her, all that her small blue-black lines on a bit of paper could not bring out.

The old woman entered and pushed me away, not harshly, but with great resolution. I saw Rameeza still bent there, sobbing, as the curtain fell between us.

My head was pounding terribly, and I thought the mud-filled passageways or the trees bent down in the storm would swallow me up. I wished I could give up my own useless life in some way that could help her. I wished I could return to the hut and the wounded woman on the bed. Ramu was by me as we walked in the rain, but both of us seemed to be shadows, changed by the dark room in which we had seen Rameeza Be.

☆   ☆   ☆

That afternoon it was dry again. The cloudburst, for that was all it had been, had blown over the city. Little Mother rested at home in the company of Swami Chari. The old man came frequently and his presence never failed to cheer her up. She showed him some pale bluish marks on the dining room wall. They were about shoulder height when one stood up. I walked in just as she was saying, "That's where Mother pasted up the Sanskrit slokas. Father had just bought the dining table, and she was worried. It was such a westernized thing to do, give up our mats and sit at a table to eat. So she wrote her favorite slokas on rice paper and stuck the paper all around the walls where we would be sure to read the characters as we ate our dinner."

The old man beamed at her. He had the copy of Sankara he'd recommended to me. He straightened up as he saw me walk in. He waved the book at me.

"Durga tells me you had a long conversation about times past last night."

"Yes, it was very calming, swamiji. But things are so hard now. I hardly feel I can see into the next minute."

"But Mira, things are improving. The curfew's been removed. They say that the birthday celebrations will come off in a spirit of goodwill. I know there are many things in our Chief Minister that are not worthy, but still . . ."

Little Mother interrupted. "How is Ramu? I saw him come in this morning. Why didn't you bring him in?"

"He was in a rush. He took me off to see old Pithulbhai's daughter."

"Pithulbhai's daughter?"

I could tell she was puzzled.

"What business has Ramu with her? How extraordinary. You know," she was addressing the swamiji now, "they tell me she keeps snakes."

Gesturing to the swamiji to sit down, she pulled up the chair she had used the night before, and set it by the window. Only now she faced the dining room. It was as if her voice and the deep past it awoke in her needed a space in which to be. The fever had cast her voice loose, and now it sped on at a momentum that could not easily be restrained.

"I didn't tell you this last night, but Mira, I had a dream in which Pithulbhai's daughter came to see me. Perhaps she thought I could help her in some way. Give her money or something. What was her name?"

"Maitreyi."

"That's right, Maitreyi! So you do know her. Well, there she was in my dream sitting in this very courtyard. Squatting by the tulasi tree she opened the little pouch at her waist and let out a snake. A real cobra! Now I had heard of such things, but I was truly amazed."

I sat up. I could not believe what I was hearing. Was this another hallucination that Little Mother had had during her fever? Or had it already happened? She often confused times and places. Part of her recuperation was to stitch the real together, heal her mind from the phantoms of her fever.

"What did she want? She really does have a snake, you know."

The two old people stared at me. I must have looked rather odd, for they moved quickly, as if something were shaking inside me, a great disturbance of soul that manifested itself in a trembling of the hands or a nervous twitch in the lips, some small sign. But I was conscious of nothing like that.

"You mean she really might have come to see me?" Little Mother spoke the words very slowly.

"Yes, perhaps she wanted help."

"Rani, Raniamma, where are you? Arre Raniamma!" the old man called out with surprising energy. He wanted to check with Rani. But Rani had left the house at great speed. She wanted to be in Sagar Talkies for the first matinee of the post-curfew season.

"She's not here." Little Mother was hesitant. "Anyway, dream or not, there she was. I can see her large as life. The snake, now that was something. It had indigo markings on it. The most beautiful creature I've seen. She said it would dance for me. Why did you go to see her, Mira? Did she ask about me?"

I still hesitated. I did not want to tell the whole truth, at least not in the presence of the swami. He was pacing up and down now with the *Vivekachudamani* in his hand. He was reading out the five hundred and seventy-fourth sloka in a loud, clear voice. As he read, it came to me slowly but with great clarity that the old man wanted to turn us away from the world in which men and women lived and breathed and moved, the world of our passions, the world of violence where whatever transcendence we might reach was fitful, flashing merely as sunlight might on a broken tile in a courtyard.

"'There is neither death nor birth, neither a bound nor a struggling soul, neither a seeker after liberation nor a liberated one—this is the ultimate truth.'"

His sonorous voice attracted Durgabai. Indeed, I could not prevent myself from listening to him. The words were magnificent in their promise that nothing existed except Brahmin. That our sufferings were illusion.

"That of course is a quotation from the *Amritabindu Upanishad*. Verbatim almost. All these distinctions are avidya, as is what you call personality."

Suddenly I was angry. I could not bear this any longer. His logic was taking us away from the only world we have, the very world of us all. If the struggle for justice was illusion, what were we? Was Rameeza nothing? Was her suffering to be emptied out, all of it relegated to mere avidya? I could not stop my tongue. I had to turn the conversation back to Maitreyi and Rameeza. Sometimes one has to speak, lest the space be filled with falsity.

"Maitreyi has a very sick woman with her. Perhaps she thought you could help her. I think she's a rape victim."

"Why didn't she bring her to me child. Of course I'll help her. You know me. Why should she fear?"

But the swamiji would not let Little Mother continue. He cut in sharply, as if neither Durgabai nor I had spoken.

"So, Mira, what did you think of your readings of Sankara?"

"Frankly, swamiji, I am very attracted to his teachings. But I found it too disturbing. Too dislocating. Even false at times, if you wish."

I fastened onto something concrete: "Didn't you tell me yourself that I shouldn't be put off by the second sloka?" I quoted it in perfect Sanskrit. I had taken the trouble to learn it by heart. There was a ferocity in my voice that he could not mistake:

"'For all beings a human birth is difficult to obtain, more so is a male body; rarer than that is Brahminhood; rarer still is the attachment to the Vedic religion.'"

I continued. "I know the sloka goes on. But I won't bother to finish it."

"But you must, child." The old man was coaxing me along. "That's the crucial bit, about how liberation is reached."

"But I'm not going to. The point as far as I'm concerned is, what do you do with a woman and one who will never be a Brahmin? What happens to her knowledge? Is she just mere pollution?"

Little Mother was shocked at my rudeness. I could tell by the flush on her face. But she kept quiet. The old swamiji was not put out. If anything he seemed kinder than before.

"I told you, Mira. Here, come and sit down. The male-female part was just a consequence of Sankara's society."

"You mean people don't think like that now? Of course they do!" I was appealing to Durgabai. "And what of the Brahminhood part? That huge system of hierarchies, it chokes out life. Meanwhile people are being beaten and molested all around us. There's terrible social injustice." I stopped short, then blurted out, "I saw a woman today. She drew a picture for me."

"What woman?"

But Ramu was standing in the room. He had just walked in. He held his finger to his mouth.

Little Mother moved forward to welcome him. Ramu bowed to her and to the swamiji. I marvelled at his ability to be courteous. I could tell he was truly pleased to see her. He was fond too of the old man. From time to time they had had long debates concerning the ontological status of the disparate body sheaths proposed by Advaita or, in a somewhat different but not wholly unrelated vein, the nature of true dialectical materialism. Ramu moved closer to me. Put his hand on my elbow to steer me away.

"Ah, I'm sorry but I must take Mira away. I wish I could stay for some tea. She may be back quite late, so you won't worry, will you, Little Mother?"

"Will you be all right child?"

There were tears in my eyes as I moved to embrace her.

CHAPTER NINE

THE HISTORY LESSON

It was late afternoon. The meeting was very crowded, and we had to press through the old gates of the schoolhouse. We entered a shed with a thatched roof, hundreds of us with hands and toes and feet and bellies pressing together. We were a whole sea of people, an ocean of us with our cries and whispers and shouts as the speeches started and red flags were thrust in the air.

There was a small girl not far from where I sat. She was just in front of Ramu, her feet crossed neatly on the matting. I saw her fist raised with everyone else's. But when she turned for an instant I saw the milky whiteness of her pupils. She was quite blind. She held a small red flag in her left hand. Ahead of us on the stage decked out with a rough paper backing were the speakers. They stood in formation, hands linked, as if part of an ancient theater. Signs of the hammer and sickle crossed over each other were painted on the paper, which rippled as the wind blew through the thatched roof. The doors swung open.

One of the speakers came forward to the microphone. He must have been a little older than I was. He reiterated the theme the others had raised. Injustice was rampant in Hyderabad, indeed in our country as a whole, in the whole world even. But we had to make a start here. Did everyone know that the Chief Minister was planning a huge birthday celebration, complete with a cardboard city, replica of the ancient inner city? Did everyone know that Limca's birthplace in the city was to be picked out in red lights in the cardboard replica? That a small child had been chosen to be Sri Krishna come dancing to Limca's birthplace?

"Myth on myth," the young man cried. "We will not be oppressed. We must rise up. After all, who is that little child? Is he not our flesh and blood? A child of the working masses."

The voices roared in approval. The next speaker was a woman from a village to the north of the city. She knew Rameeza Be's family. She started by speaking of the atrocities committed every day. Just the day before, five peasants were slaughtered before dawn. They had refused to pay taxes to the landlord. Two sisters were raped and buried half alive in the shifting sands off the Arabian Sea. For fear of molestation nurses were terrified to take up their duties in the far-flung villages. Listening to her voice my ears grew swollen, like wheat filled with water, afloat on a swamp. I felt my body stuck in its place. I could barely lift my hand to push back the strands of hair that were crowding into my eyes. In a daze I listened to the long list of atrocities.

"Now here she comes, the woman herself," the voice cried.

There were loud chants in the room as old Maitreyi hobbled in. She was dressed just as we had seen her, in dark blue rags. But the end of her sari covered her face almost completely. I wouldn't have been surprised if the snake was still hidden in her waistband. Maitreyi was led to the loudspeaker and she spoke in simple language, spluttering a little. I had not known until then that she was a witness. She had come in the late evening to sweep out the police station. It was an unusual time but with a daughter-in-law about to give birth she was worried about making it in the next morning. Hearing a commotion she had hidden behind a gooseberry bush a little to the right of the main entrance. She had watched as Rameeza was dragged up the steps. Outside in the yard lay the badly beaten corpse of Muhammad, Rameeza's husband.

Unable to prevent herself, the old woman had followed the policemen into the building. In clear detail she described as best she could the brutality of the rape: how as Rameeza's sari was torn from her body, a whole line of policemen still wearing their boots scrabbled among themselves for who should go first; how her wild fistblows, her sharp cries for help had subsided as blood filled her wounds and ran down her bruised mouth, her blackened eyes. Afterward Rameeza was thrown into the cell. With no one to see her, the old woman had edged forward to comfort her, gently parting her split lips, ladling in a few drops of water. It seemed to Maitreyi that Rameeza could feel nothing at all, had willed herself to part company with her violated body for a little while. "Aaaiou, aaiou," the old woman cried out, raising her fists in the air, tearing at her own clothing.

People leaped up in the crowd and shouted for revenge. A man came on stage. Quite firmly he led old Maitreyi to the side.

"The time for revenge is past," he cried out. "It is time for action. The spontaneous violence we directed against the police station must be channelled carefully. We must act, my friends."

But his voice was lost in the general stampede onto the stage. Various members of the crowd had their own story to tell. Maitreyi seemed to have shrunk into a hole. I wondered where Rameeza was. Was she all alone in the company of the musclebound kabbadi man? I had a sudden urge to push out through the huge crowd and find her.

But the next speaker was on the stage, tall and thin, her lean body covered in a black sari. Her face was cut with lines. She was introduced as Rosamma from the hill country. She led the great cry that swept the room:

"Overcome oppression, down with chains."

She spoke of knives and bombs, of a great cleansing that was necessary. A thousand voices rose:

"Down with chains, take up the knife of justice!"

My mouth felt dry. I looked for Ramu, but there was someone in between us and I couldn't see his face. I thought I heard his voice in the great vortex of sound that swept up to the thatched roof and swirled to all the corners of the city. I heard my voice too, but it did not belong to me anymore. I let the cry ring through my ears. I felt I had fallen, vanished, and that my soul, a tiny thing in red skirts, had danced out between my toes and raced away. I longed to run, to flee the dark room and the chanting voices, but I was firmly welded in place.

At the very end of the meeting, as people were trickling out, Ramu stood by me again. There was a strange light in his eyes. The tall woman in black stood beside him. Rosamma tapped me on the shoulder.

"So you are Mira."

I nodded at her. She looked at me with a small smile, as if sensing my fear.

"I know your mother's family. Your grandmother was a great woman. You must not be afraid to use knives. How else should we reach the new world?"

Someone called her away. Ramu and I left together. On the way back we found a small bar on Nampally Road and went in. The beggars were still in the temple courtyard. The air was growing dark with rain clouds again. Nothing had changed. We sat on the rickety balcony of Mohan's Bar and ordered two beers. The stench of sawdust was in my nostrils, sawdust filled with alcohol and spittle. I could still feel the crowd at the meeting pressing against my arms and legs. My hands trembled as I sat in the metal chair. The slight breeze that blew in from the Public Gardens did not calm me.

I pushed forward against Ramu so that the table lurched.

"Listen to me. Who should I turn my knife against? Little Mother because she lives in a big house? Rani? Laura? Myself?"

"Shh-shh." He held his fingers to his lips. The men at the next table were listening.

"Be warned," he whispered. There was an odd quality to his voice almost as if he wished the whole world to hear. "This is my last existence. I shall not come again."

I was suddenly frightened.

"Ramu, you have to talk to me. I mean it. Where shall we live? We will live together, won't we?"

He held my wrist. The drops of moisture trembled on the cold glasses filled with golden beer. There were children crying in the street below us.

"We shall live in the streets, my love. Like beggars, like birds! Waiter, waiter, over here."

He pitched his voice higher, as if he were singing now. When the waiter came he ordered two more beers. I still had not finished mine. The men at the next table were laughing, a rough belly laugh. They had plastic briefcases next to them. I looked into the street below. The children were playing in a ring around the Gandhi statue. The high steps of the post office behind them looked utterly deserted.

In the distance, beyond the Divine Life Temple, beyond the white painted walls of our college, I could make out the bits and pieces of the cardboard city that was being erected for the Chief Minister's birthday. There were high rods of steel and wire dangling with light bulbs in a multitude of colors. There were painted placards being pulled into place and cut stalks of the palmyra and vine knotted into the shapes of triumphal arches. As we watched it all, the slight mist veiling it, the colors of the setting sun pouring over it, the unreal city seemed part of another world, another life. What did we have to do with it?

I thought I felt Rosamma's thin fingers on my shoulder. It was uncanny. Down on the street below was a truck full of women. They were women construction workers who had been brought in from the villages. The truck was making its way toward the Public Gardens. It ground to a halt almost in front of us, under the lights that spelled Mohan's Bar. I looked down. Tired women were clambering onto the truck. They poured out of the street behind us. They had sickles and knives in their hands. All day they had worked on the arcades that lined Nampally Road. Now they had more work ahead of them. The entire cardboard city had to be ready by daybreak tomorrow.

A thin woman wearing a red sari got on. She might have been Rosamma's sister. She had the same proud bearing, the same set to her shoulders. She was young, very young, though. She was the last to climb in. Her blouse was half open. She knotted it at the waist. Then as the truck started, she raised her sickle in her right hand and leaned over the edge. A thin line of spittle fell from her lips and evaporated in the light. It was red in that light, as though she had been chewing paan, or as if blood had flowed from her mouth. She stood straight now, clutching the sides of the truck that gathered speed as it roared off toward the Public Gardens. There was something lonely and proud and fearless about her. Her face was still, utterly set in that light. I saw a hawk from the temple fly low, make circles around her head. Ramu was watching her too. The truck moved out of sight, and bicycles and rickshaws filled the street.

What was in Ramu's mind? I felt a great emptiness in the pit of me, a nausea compounded by fear, cowardice perhaps. Then suddenly an image clarified for me. I wanted to tell him. I was starting to understand.

"Ramu, I think she's running away, my soul. A tiny child. Look, her red skirts are flashing."

He looked sad, as if there might forever be a lack in me he could hardly heal.

"Mira, can't you look at things straight? Didn't you see that working woman in the truck? All those women. That's the truth, I tell you. Why is it so hard for you? How can you ever write properly unless you do?"

But I wanted to make him see what I saw. I loved him, but he had to see me as I was.

"The self is always two. Always broken. Don't you see that, Ramu? Or can't your politics take that? Look, given the world as it is, there's nowhere people like us can be whole. The best I can do is leapfrog over the cracks in the earth, over the black fissures. From one woman's body into another. From this Mira that you know into Little Mother, into Rameeza, into Rosamma, into that woman in the truck on the way to the Public Gardens. A severed head, a heart, a nostril with a breathing hole, a breast, a bloodied womb. What are we?"

"My soul and I," he whispered.

"Yes, yes." I hurried on. I had to make him understand. I touched the glass beaded with moisture. I set a little of the beer to my mouth. It tasted flat, salty—Golconda beer.

But he was angry now and ignored the bartender who came out with a filthy bit of paper on which he had scribbled the bill.

"OK, Saab. OK? OK?" The man was addressing Ramu.

"There's something you don't see, Mira."

"What?"

"We don't even have a pin or a bit of string or a rope to hold us together. Not you and me. Not us."

He threw out his arms. In the street beneath, children were throwing stones at the Gandhi statue, trying to dislodge a pair of mating pigeons. The children had made up a jingle. I could not catch the words, though they were singing it loudly.

"Remember how we used to say 'With a broken stick, a stone, a piece of glass, we'll build it all up again'?"

I nodded, mutely.

"Well, we're not building. We're just standing here useless, letting him get on with it. Sawdust, caged beasts, nizams, children, we'll all be sucked into death soon enough."

I wanted to touch him. I was no longer angry. I needed to hold him, lower him into me. But I couldn't. There was nowhere to go. No elsewhere.

"You think we'll all be in storybooks, don't you. But whose story, Mira? Look at that poor old man. Gandhi, I mean. Turn around and look, for god's sake. He's an island now. We race around him and leave him where he is. When he's picked up it's to embellish our own tales."

Ramu's voice took on another edge. He was mimicking a child in school, then the schoolmistress.

"So familiar, but who is he, Miss?"

Ramu leaned back in his chair and struck a pose. He adjusted the imaginary spectacles on his nose. Held up his hands as if motioning a class to silence.

"Mohandas Karamchand Gandhi. Who's that, Miss? Born . . . died... receptacle of pigeon shit."

I drank my beer hurriedly. I wanted to get him away before he drank too much. Before his craziness got into him.

"Ramu, shhh."

He couldn't stop now. He was enjoying himself too much. The two men at the neighboring table were staring at us.

"Who's the Nizam, Miss? . . .

"Her chalk squeaks on the board. Descended from the great northern mountains in the year. . . on a white charger named Sundar. Lived in the palace which is now our national museum. Adored rubies and diamonds and blackbirds. Sent hundreds to death. Forced men to leap into boiling water to pick up pearls with their teeth. They lost their skins. . .

"Ah Miss, who's Gandhi? Ah Miss, what's this Gandhi good for? I want to be like the Nizam. . .

"Who's that, Miss? That's Limca Gowda, the great ruler of Hyderabad. Chief Minister. The child starts clapping. Yes, that's right, child. He's the Founder of the Great Hydroelectric Project, Founder of the Ever Ready Brigade, Mender of All Wounds. Father of Hyderabad! End of Lesson."

The two men had returned to their drinks. They were laughing out loud at some joke. Had they heard Ramu to the end? He was hot and flushed. The bartender was impatient. I gave him the few rupees I had with me and helped Ramu stand up. He was quite straight and tall and made me walk ahead of him down the narrow twisting stairs of Mohan's Bar and Restaurant. The stench of urine was intense at the foot of the stairs. We hurried out. Directly ahead of us the college lay utterly dark. There was no one we knew in sight.

☆　☆　☆

That night I decided to stay with Ramu in his hotel room. Somehow I could not bear to leave him. First I called home, and when Rani picked up the phone I told her I was staying with a cousin in Gowliguda. She said she would pass the message onto Little Mother, who was not at home. She had gone to the clinic. "Her patients needed her, she said." There was a slight sneer in Rani's voice, then a growing excitement.

She had heard that Dharam, the great film star, hero of *Isak Katha*, would be coming to the birthday celebrations in the Public Gardens. "He will be singing the song of praise, first of all. It will be a history of the nation!" Laura had put aside her packing for Canada, and she was going to accompany Rani to the Public Gardens. I was thankful to be able to put the phone down to stop listening to Rani.

The hotel room was small, with plaster peeling in the corners where the rain had dripped down. There was a small attached bathroom. Ramu went in to take a shower. When he came back he had a lungi wrapped around him. His body was wet with the shower water.

We sat together at the edge of the narrow metal bed and looked out over the balcony. It was growing dark. The hills were smoky in the distance, and the Public Gardens where the cardboard city rose had all but vanished into the blur of mist that swept up from the river at night. The lights from the placards were small prickles of color, bleeding into one another. There was the scent of wood fires burning beneath us. If we had been born into another lifetime, all this might have been like paradise. I couldn't resist a feeling of pleasure as I sat by him.

Sometimes I felt I wanted to live with Ramu and have children and all that. But I knew that a steady life would have been very hard for him. And did I really want to cook and sew and keep house? I shrugged the thought off. The wood fires in the distance were tinged with the scent of spices boiling over. I imagined mothers preparing the night's food, their small children racing about barefoot. Rice and a little dal and a few chilies. Perhaps some extra vegetables if they were lucky. What would it be like to be surrounded by one's children? Would I feel I was born again? But their needs would clamor at my ears. Those little cries would be terribly loud. I would have to stick my fingers in my ears.

Ramu was gazing ahead of him. Between the dark hills and the high road the river was faintly visible, a gray line, a fluidity that separated land from land. The river had been there for a thousand, two thousand years. Kingdoms had risen and fallen about those banks. Others had sat at a distance and looked through the dim light at the waters. Lovers had sat like us, side by side smelling the scent of wood fires, gazing down. How quiet it was now.

I knew that once the river had been a thoroughfare and that most of the traffic now conducted on the high roads and over bridges had been carried by water. In the fourteenth and fifteenth centuries the water was thick with silver sails. Then came a terrible carnage. Thousands of dead elephants were flung into the waters. The river rose, thick red. Whole cities perished.

Then a hundred years passed, two hundred, shorter spans of time. A stallion dipped its bleeding hooves in water. A seagull circled overhead, its feathers shot with light. A dying prince floated down the river, his body covered in sackcloth and ashes to trick the enemy. He died a safe death, in another kingdom, under the gentle shade of a tamarind tree.

Then British barges floated down the river, the men odd looking, ears covered in stiff caps, pink cheeks puffing as the wind stung them. The women were scrupulously veiled, head to toe. Eyes that had gazed at daffodils and dilated in Derbyshire fogs, narrowed now in the harsh sun of Hyderabad. The ladies kept their palms away from water. The gentlemen chewed tobacco and grunted at the bearers to move the guns. The crates at the back of the boat were laden with watches, screws, tins of tea.

Time slipped. A knot in a river's throat. Rocks, guns, grenades. At nightfall boats docked at the Pakeezah steps. It was the freedom struggle. Stubby fingers, sweaty arms delved under sacking, under mounds of rotting fish and straw, reaching for cool metal. Then hidden in sherwani and sari the armaments found their way to safe houses and were held in readiness for use against the British.

As I sat by Ramu in the low depression on the thin mattress, my mind moved away. Here we were in our new world, our hotel room. The land lay below, smoky in the dusk. Ramu too seemed far away. His right hand lay on mine. He let it rest like that, our two hands touching, the color of the skin almost transparent, a dark brown in the light that came from the road. Like petals of the same bloom, or fruits of the same tree.

There was a loud knocking on the door, and a little boy brought in plates of food and set them on the table. It was quite dark by now, but we did not turn on the light. We did not eat. That night he told me what he wanted to do. He said his comrades in the party would help. I trembled as I lay in his arms. I felt our life was ending. He had never been so gentle.

"This is Hotel Brindavan, isn't it?" he teased me. "It's Lord Krishna's kingdom. It's time to make love." He smoothed the hair away from my cheek and kissed me. There was a darkness in him, a bitter iron. It entered me then and it has never left.

"Think of Krishna coming to the battlefield." He rolled over on his side as he spoke. My back was against the cool wall. "When Arjun saw him his hair stood on end. All the worlds rolled into his great mouth, flaming. Time was no more."

We were both naked that night and the cool breeze fanned us. It rolled off the river and the plains and the high-walled, decrepit city. I felt the grandeur of his vision. But I could not see where it could lead. I saw the old woman again, Maitreyi, in her crumpled blue sari, hunched before the microphone, then her body shrinking into the great crowd. That crowd could erupt into sheer rage. I saw Rameeza's bruised cheeks. I wanted to melt into Ramu, to curl up with him forever and ever in a nest of skin and bone. I wanted to draw him into me, and have us born again and again, in one life after the next, holding each other.

Next morning we were up before sunrise. I hastily put away my little odds and ends. Ramu wanted me to leave before anyone arrived on the scene. He felt he would be watched very closely. I embraced him quickly and walked out onto the stone staircase of Hotel Brindavan. It was early morning, an hour before dawn, and already Nampally Road was filled with life.

CHAPTER TEN

CARDBOARD CITY

I felt very calm that morning as I walked through the sunlit streets of Hyderabad and found my way back along Nampally Road. The gates of Little Mother's house lay open as if the inhabitants were either utterly innocent of the turbulence all around or had fled the city. No one was in sight. My room looked as if it had just been swept. But nothing was disturbed in it. It was clear and cool. I entered and looked through the window. In the abandoned graveyard a torn kite hung from a stone. The paper was unnaturally pale, bleached with the water from the storm that had emptied the sky.

Clear sunshine shone onto my unused bed and onto the pages of the lined notebook that lay open against the pillow. I glanced at the few lines I had written the day before the police station had burned. It was a description of the courtyard outside the other window: colors of the paving stones, the motion of leaves as the sparrows rose from the bush, the pallor of a cabbage butterfly hovering over lemongrass. A series of factual descriptions with a certain lyrical note, but nothing special. The kind of writing where one tries one's hand, where the voice hasn't found itself. It seemed so distant now, so unreal. I could not believe I had really written those lines. Who was I really?

I shut the book with a snap and set it on the neatly folded cloth with all my other notebooks. Pile on pile of an autobiography I would never write. Perhaps someday I would burn all those papers! I straightened the books I had left on the desk and picked up a pair of chappals. The soles were coming apart. I slipped off the chappals I was wearing and put the old ones on. The leather was soft underfoot. My actions were all simple and abrupt. The practical part of my mind was working, carefully, slowly, leading me forward. I changed my sari and blouse, closed the shutters so the hot sun of noonday would not enter, and walked into the courtyard. There was still no sign of Little Mother. I thought I heard Rani's voice on the balcony of Laura's house but I couldn't be sure.

Outside, the street was unnaturally still. The shops were all shut, it was a state holiday. A torn poster from the movie next door flew past on the street. Most of the space on the poster was taken up by a triangle made of blocks of irregular shapes latched together. The whole thing was printed in black, and near the top left-hand side was the image of a small boy, Isaac, clutching a rock for dear life. *Isak Katha,* it said in big letters, starring Swarna Dharam as Ibrahim. I kicked it over and watched it blow away.

Outside Optical Palace I felt my chappal give way. I knew that if I were lucky, just a few feet farther on I might find a cobbler. Why had I put on the old chappals anyway? Did I want to be stopped in my tracks? Did I want to walk barefoot? A longing for Ramu gripped me. I stood utterly still on the pavement, then forced myself to go on.

As I approached the crossroads by the Gandhi statue I saw the wooden begging bowls and tin pots the beggars had dropped. Late at night, when I was in Hotel Brindavan with Ramu, the beggars who lived outside the small Shiva temple were rounded up by the special police. They were dragged into black vans and driven to the outskirts of the city, then forced out into the ruins of the old fort. Someone had calculated that it would take them a day and a half to walk back, and by then the great celebrations would be over. Hyderabad had to be kept beautiful, so the big signs said, posted all over the walls and pinned to the trees. Attached to the top of each poster was a photo of the Chief Minister holding a small boy's hand.

The Divine Life Temple was empty, and I saw a few of the devotees, crouching by the gates. Next to them stood a handful of Jehovah's Witnesses. They looked so odd, shipwrecked where they were, behind the blue painted gates of the temple. They held copies of *The Watchtower* in their hands, a journal printed in Brooklyn, a tall towering form scrawled in black ink on the cover. A few days earlier they had hit the city like a rash, proclaiming the end of the world, waving copies of their yellow pamphlets. They had found support in the Krishna devotees, who took to the streets with their cymbals and drums, crying "O Vrindavan is here, rejoice all." But how could the devotees and the *Watchtower* folk keep company? Or was it that they all felt time was drawing to a close and, infected with Limca's fervor, felt compelled to unmake all that stood? Did our lives seem so pitiful to them? I could not tell.

I was relieved to see the cobbler I knew a little farther along. As I moved over to the pavement where she squatted I realized that behind me, at a distance of about ten yards or so, was the first of a slow-moving convoy of lorries packed with cheering villagers. The lorries were bound for the Public Gardens. Soon the stadium and the cardboard city would be surrounded by villagers and townspeople. An ocean of people would encircle the glittering pageant, and Limca's birthday party would begin.

I felt cold and sick at heart. I lifted up my sari a few inches and showed the cobbler the broken chappal. She was an old woman. She bent over my chappal, scrutinizing it. She was suffering from leukoderma and her face was a patchwork of colors, ordinary brown skin bitten with the raw pink that the disease made. A knot of white hair was tied to the nape of her neck with cobbler's thread. It fell to one side with its own weight, and I could see in the clear morning light the fine sculpted bones of her neck and jaw. When she looked up at me the sunlight strained through the hair, lending her an unearthly beauty.

How carefully she worked. Just for an instant she looked up as the first of the trucks with its load of cheering villagers drove by. "Limca is our father," they sang out in tired voices. Some of them had been travelling all night. They had been enticed to the city with the promise of three free meals and a handful of rupees. The penalties for refusing were harsh. There was so little room in some of the trucks that few people could sit. So they stood for the long ride, packed upright against each other, men and women and a whole horde of small children. Some of the larger children rode in a separate truck. They waved small replicas of the national flag. But instead of Gandhi's symbol of the spinning wheel at the center of the tricolor, these flags had Limca Gowda's face, a simplified silhouette, but unmistakable, a craggy blackened thing.

I knelt on the pavement by the cobbler woman as the trucks raced by. I could feel Nampally Road shake under the burden. She seemed not to notice. How carefully she worked. First she undid a thread that held my chappal together at its base. Then she laid out the slivers of leather on a stone by her side. The heel was completely worn out and needed to be rebuilt. With her two-inch chisel she cut fresh slivers of leather from a thick scrap at her side. There were people in the street now, walking at a brisk pace, but I was so intent on her work that I did not notice their faces.

She must have worked with great concentration for half an hour at least, her neck bent over the broken chappal. I was watching her thread her needle to fix the toehold that had snapped when I sensed a heavy boot beside me. I glanced up into the glare of a torchlight. It was a man in dark fatigues, the Ever Ready uniform. His torch blinded me as I stumbled up.

"Name, address," he snapped.

"Mira Kannadical." I saw no harm in giving him my real name, then added a false address, one that could hurt no one. It was the number of the Sagar Talkies.

"Occupation?" He scribbled down some notes as I explained what I did for a living. I felt nervous for the old woman cobbler, for the man seemed to have lost interest in me. He stared at her, kicked some of her leather scraps into the gutter, and then walked away, lathi in hand. I bent over the trickle of water, picking up the leather. The old woman was composed as she watched me, her hand still holding the needle. Her body was so calm on that thin strip of pavement. But I felt the passion rise in me: it was all so senseless. Just a flicker of anger, and the Ever Ready man could have kicked her into the gutter and hauled me off with him. It would have been too late before anyone we knew heard anything at all. I watched her face but said nothing, then thanking her I paid her for her labor. I could feel the strength of her hands in my newly made chappals as I walked firmly toward the Public Gardens.

I wandered in from the back where just a handful of soldiers stood, laughing and cracking open peanuts. Their bayonets were propped harmlessly by them. They hardly noticed me, a thin woman in a cotton sari carrying a cloth bag. I could have been any one of a hundred people, any one of a thousand in a crowd.

☆ ☆ ☆

It was damp at the edge of the field. I squatted, watching the last-minute preparations. The pedestal and the surrounding high platforms were all fixed. The stage was painted in the colors of the flag, green, white, and orange. There was a tall palm tree and a model of the charka. Someone had wheeled in a giant cutout of Gandhi. For some reason it was locked with clumsy chains to one of the Prime Minister with her immaculate hair-do, a lock of white hair regally brushed back. And next to them, largest of all, was a silhouette of the Chief Minister, dressed in make-believe khadi glittering with sequins. In its right hand the Limca image held a torch, an Ever Ready light. I gathered this would be the theme of the celebration: a new light in darkness, a brightness in history, Limca Gowda!

Already children dressed in sparkling costumes were being led in. Several would participate in the pageant illustrating stages in Limca's life. Watching them I was gripped by a vertiginous sense of the unreal, a nausea so strong that I thought I would slip and fall. I steadied myself against the earth, trying to keep my balance. The sunlight was clear and I tried to see things as they were. They were remaking history, tampering with the ordinary truth, distorting things as they actually were. An unreal thing was being clamped onto us that could choke us to death.

Slowly I turned my back. Moving away to the outer edge of the field, I stumbled upon the path that Ramu had showed me so long ago, the path by the magnolia trees that led to the pond. The trees were shaking out their moisture. Even the air was different here, far from the preparations for the pageant. I could feel the rough grass curl over my toes.

I recalled with a small shock that mother had once brought me here when I was five years old. We were visiting Hyderabad. There were booths crowded onto the stubble, black awnings, cascades of balloons, tinsel and torches lighting the faces of countless children and their parents. I had rested with mother by the side of a red painted booth. I could almost hear again the clear, tinkling music. I searched for the two chalk cliffs near the river. But they were long gone, blasted out for chalk. The land near the river was flat now, a dull beige color, pocked with small huts. And there was no booth near me. The field ahead was almost bare. Out of my memory I heard a cry:

"Fields of paradise. Three paise entry!"

A clown with a bauble at the tip of his nose had waddled toward us. When his wide black pants caught in the stubble, he laughed out loud. There were two balloons in his hand. I rubbed my eyes. They hurt me. The sunlight was growing stronger.

Then I heard the sound of laughter behind me. Far away from the cardboard city and the great jostling crowds at the other end of the Public Gardens a man was pushing his bicycle. A woman walked beside him, a small child at her hip. She raised the baby to the sunlight and it laughed out loud, a rich gurgling sound. Behind them was the lotus pool. I had forgotten it, but it came back to me now. Delicate golden bloom flashed behind them. A crate full of tomatoes, wired to the back of the bicycle wobbled a little as the man walked. A little girl with pigtails and pink ribbons in her hair was seated on the metal rod that ran from the seat to the handlebars. She looked straight ahead of her, filled with pride. They were all going somewhere, they had a life of their own. The man leaned over now, tickling the belly of the older child. The bicycle swerved to the right and as the children screamed with laughter, the father set it straight again. The woman put out her hand and held onto the tomatoes, which were threatening to spill out.

I stood there and watched that clear picture of life, with an ache I could not help. It hurt. They were figures of flesh and water and light. I felt thrust out, evicted from joy. My own family were strangers to me. And the thought of bringing children into this world seemed too hard. I lacked a natural life. What did I have but this confusion and rage?

But I felt I had not erred. Perhaps in another existence I could know that sheer life, the wet glisten of leaf on a small child's cheek, a voice so pure that it cut the air. I walked out of the Public Gardens feeling frail but clean, freed of longings I could not satisfy. I pushed forward into the large crowds gathering impatiently for the great event.

Somehow I found a space where I could stand at the edge of the platform that bore the cardboard city. Its domes and minarets, its winding streets and bridges, rivalled our own. Where was Hyderabad to be seen in this glittering fiction that swept us out of our lives into a time about to be?

To the sound of trumpets and horns, to the clatter of horseback riders and the slow stately processional of elephants, the Chief Minister approached. He was dressed in a shimmering tunic of antique cut. A sword hung at his side. He sat on a marble chair that was drawn up in front of the cardboard city. Now the pageant of his life could begin.

First the lights shone on the right of the stage. It was a small village in the south. Limca's birth was depicted. His poor mother who had labored in the fields with sweat running off her back lay down in a hut and gave birth. The cries of the actress mimicking labor mingled with the roar of the crowd.

Next, on a dais I saw a small child sitting straight in a chair. A seven-year-old. He held a metal bowl in his hand. "Mother," he said in a clear voice magnified by the loudspeakers, "Mother, take my grains of rice. The country is in need. I will not eat." As the arc lights shone on him the small boy was uncomfortable. He twitched in his chair. Rouge burned his cheek. It was the second part of the pageant.

After each phase of Limca's life there were patriotic songs sung by a chorus from the local schools. The soldiers on guard at the edge of the platform raised their guns in salute. The plainclothesmen saluted. Later, the film stars of *Isak Katha*, accompanied by a small Sri Krishna, were scheduled to descend the great stairway that ran down the three-story city. They would approach Limca and sing his praises. But that was yet to come.

It was the freedom struggle now and Limca was a young man of twenty, making a huge profit selling guns and soda right under the noses of the British. This part of the pageant was paid for by the Junior Chamber of Commerce, and their green and gold banners hung over the arcades at the side. As the action went on, Jayalatha, the famous playback singer, warbled out in high-pitched notes a song with the lilting moral "Develop the Nation's Entrepreneurship." It was set to a well-known film song and no one had trouble following. There was wild cheering at the end and the stage filled with whirring lights.

But the marble chair looked heavier suddenly, and the Chief Minister wiped sweat from his forehead. He looked older too, as if the makeup had started peeling from his face. The sets were being changed for the next event. Stagehands and security men ran back and forth. As I tried to shift forward to get a better view I heard a crackling sound high up in the pinnacle of the cardboard city, close to where the staircase rose. Then, without further warning, a sheet of flame whipped down, a falling wave of fire that licked at the stage behind Limca.

There was a great cry as something exploded inside the cardboard city and a thousand sheets of paper and wire and bulbs all held together by immense human labor started to burn. Sucked by a great wind, the blaze rose high in the air and the flames could not be held back. There was scuffling, screams, moans from human beings who were being trampled by others, gunshots, sharp cries, sirens, and the bark of police dogs suddenly unleashed. I was being pushed by the great crowd.

All around me I saw men, women, children, society matrons, soldiers, sailors, peasants, princes of state, poor sweepers of latrines, children who lived off the droppings they found in the street. There was no distinction of class, creed, or caste as we shoved in a mass of arms and legs, mouths and bellies, out of the immense metal gates of the Public Gardens. Trying to free myself of that welter of shared life, beating hearts, bent heads, thighs streaked with mud, I half-slipped, then steadied myself as I glimpsed flames dancing on the lotus pool.

The water was burning! A fire had been lit in water. I could not suppress that thought. Now I had no power to stop anything. I knew a heavy rain must fall.

Somehow I got back home. The gates had been torn down by the rioting crowd. I ran into the living room. Little Mother was there with some bandages in her hand. She looked at me quizzically.

"Ramu was just here looking for you. He was covered in oil and blood."

That's all she said. She asked no questions. Tears flowed out of my eyes. So he was still alive. Then I sensed someone in the dark corner by the Ganapati statue. Who was it? Not Ramu surely? As I moved forward the figure advanced. A woman. I knew her from real life and from my dreams. A young woman, almost my age, her head covered in an old sari. Her eyes were as dark as the soot that fell from the city of cardboard. I touched her hurt hand.

"Why don't you sit, child? Rameeza has been waiting for you. Maitreyi brought her here." Little Mother was so gentle. I sat on the stone floor, utterly quiet. There was gunfire outside. I could smell the bitter odor of tear gas. Our walls were crumbling. I looked at Rameeza. She edged closer to me. Her mouth was healing slowly.

ABOUT THE AUTHOR

Born in India in 1951, Meena Alexander was raised in India and North Africa. Her poems have appeared in numerous journals, including *Chelsea, Nimrod,* and *The Massachusetts Review.* She is the author of the volumes of poetry *House of a Thousand Doors* (Three Continents Press, Washington DC, 1988); and *The Storm: A Poem in Five Parts* (Red Dust, New York, 1989).

Author of the critical study *Women in Romanticism: Mary Wollstonecraft, Dorothy Wordsworth and Mary Shelley* (MacMillan, London, 1989/Barnes and Noble, Lanham MD, 1989), Alexander is particularly interested in contemporary Indian feminism and postcolonial issues. She has written the introduction to *Truth Tales,* a collection of short stories by contemporary Indian women (Feminist Press, New York, 1990), and her work is included in several anthologies, such as *Making Waves, Writing by Asian Women* (Beacon Press, Boston, 1989), and *Contemporary Indian Poetry* (Ohio State University Press, 1990). Her memoirs, entitled *Fault Lines,* will be published by Feminist Press in 1992.

In 1988 Alexander was writer in residence at the Center for American Cultural Studies at Columbia University. She currently teaches in the writing program at Columbia University and at Hunter College and the Graduate Center, City University of New York. She lives in New York City with her husband and two children.

photo: Tom McWilliam